The Poodle Who Picked Pockets

A Grandpa Max Tall Tale

By Lynn Franklin

Copyright

The Poodle Who Picked Pockets
by Lynn Franklin
© 2018 by Lynn Franklin

Franklin & Franklin Publishing

eBook ISBN: 978-0-9855457-8-9
Print ISBN: 978-0-9855457-7-2

Also by Lynn Franklin

Jeweler's Gemstone Mystery Series

The Blue Diamond
The Pirate's Ruby
The Carolina Emerald

Readers' Specials

The Diamond Digest

Want more fun stories?
Go to www.LynnFranklin.com to join The
Diamond Digest

Lynn@LynnFranklin.com.

DEDICATION

To the grandparents everywhere who make the world a special place. And to the children who love them.

CONTENTS

THE POODLE WHO PICKED POCKETS

"Are you sure Santa knows I'm staying here tonight?" Six-year-old Kimberley West clutched Mr. Bear, her well-worn teddy bear, and gazed up at her grandfather.

"Of course." Max Hershey tugged his granddaughter's ponytail. "Santa knows everything."

Kim scowled. "But sometimes he forgets. He forgot my puppy last year."

Max cast about for an appropriate answer.

Kim had been asking for a puppy ever since

she could walk. Two years ago, after meeting a standard poodle on the boardwalk, her request became more specific: She'd like a standard poodle puppy, please.

As Max later explained to his daughter, Tina, the breed did seem perfect for an only child. Smart, friendly and easily trainable, poodles tended to be wonderful with children. And, given that Tina and husband Nick were school teachers, they had summers free to take the puppy to training classes.

He'd never forget the pained expression on Tina's face as she explained that they couldn't afford a dog, let alone a pure-bred puppy.

Puppies cost money, not only the initial investment, but also the subsequent care. The annual outlay of vet bills, food, toys, training tools and the like added up.

Most school teachers, Tina had said, supplemented their low teaching salaries by accepting other jobs during the summer. She and Nick had opted to spend summers with their only child. They simply couldn't afford a dog.

Max immediately offered to buy the puppy. But Tina, the most independent of his four daughters, refused his help.

Kim was young, Tina had said, and would soon move on to other desires.

But she didn't. That year "standard poodle puppy" topped Kim's list for Santa Claus.

Though she'd quietly accepted her other gifts, Max ached to see her disappointment.

She'd continued to lobby for a puppy and, last year, the only item on her Christmas list was "standard poodle puppy."

When Christmas morning dawned with no puppy, Kim promptly proclaimed Santa either didn't exist or was a very bad man for making promises he didn't keep.

Max wanted to tell Kim the truth about Santa and explain why Kim's family couldn't afford a dog right now.

Kim's parents agreed. But Max's other daughters squelched the idea, arguing that there were other grandchildren to consider. If Kim decided Santa didn't exist, they said, she'd tell her cousins and ruin Christmas for everyone.

To Max's horror, his daughters launched a "Santa is good" campaign, bombarding Kim with "proof" in the form of magazine articles, photos and movies.

Kim sullenly listened to her aunts and cousins. She eventually dropped the topic of Santa completely and everyone breathed a sigh of relief.

Everyone, that is, except Max.

He knew his most precocious grandchild would focus on the problem until she produced her own explanation.

Kim's theory, however, surprised even him.

Last month, when the grandchildren started making their lists for Santa, Kim asked permission to spend Christmas Eve with her grandparents.

The idea of hosting a grandchild on Christmas Eve thrilled Max's wife Irene. She'd immediately drafted a list of special foods and games to make the evening memorable.

Max, however, had been suspicious.

Kim frequently "helped" in his jewelry store and stayed the night.

So why did she suddenly want to spend Christmas Eve with them?

"You have a chimney, we don't," Kim had replied.

Seeing the confused expression on his face, she'd explained.

"Everyone says Santa comes into the house through the chimney. We don't have a chimney."

"But you've always found presents under the tree on Christmas morning. So Santa must have found a way in."

Kim had nodded. "But he's never brought my puppy. Maybe he needs a chimney to bring the puppy."

And so here she was, bundled up in flannel pjs, glasses perched on her nose, messy ponytail spread on her pillow. What was he going to say when she woke up to find no puppy?

Swallowing the lump in his throat, Max forced a smile.

"How 'bout a bed time story?"

"Yes, please." Kim tucked Mr. Bear under the blanket with her, arranging it so the stuffed bear's head peered out.

"I know you like to hear true stories," Max said. "But given that it's Christmas, don't you think Mr. Bear would like to hear a funny story, maybe about poodles?"

"Is it real?"

"Well, all stories are based on reality. I'm just going to embellish it a bit."

For a moment, Kim stared up at him. Then a smile spread over her face.

"You like to make up stories, don't you, Grandpa?"

"I'm just thinking of Mr. Bear." He patted the stuffed bear's head.

Kim giggled.

"So do you want to hear the poodle story?"

"Yes, please."

"Once upon a time. . ."

Once upon a time, in a town very like our own, a standard poodle and a long-haired dachshund learned to talk to people. Now before you say "My dog talks to me," we're not referring to the "mama" sound some pugs can make or the "ah-roo-roo" reference to "cookie" or "bathroom." Sam the poodle and Tucker the dachshund could actually form human words.

And why, you might rightly ask, would they bother to do that? After all, throughout the ages dogs have done quite well manipulating their people without resorting to conversation. Witness the modern dog who spends his days lolling on the sofa, barking at the mailman or annoying the family cat – all in exchange for enthusiastically wagging his tail when his people returned home from work.

Such a life bored the poodle and dachshund to tears. They yearned for a real job.

But not one of the traditional dog jobs of hunting, herding or guarding. Nor were they interested in chasing fuzzy lures around race tracks, running obstacle courses or entering beauty pageants.

What Sam and Tucker most wanted in the whole wide world was to become detectives.

Tucker envisioned himself as the Nero Wolfe half of the team. When not consulting with the chef about breakfast, lunch and dinner, he would sit behind a large desk and instruct his assistant – that would be Sam – on how to conduct the investigation. Eventually, while puffing on a good cigar, Tucker would call everyone together and announce the solution.

As the Archie part of the pair, Sam in no

way considered himself Tucker's employee. They were, by golly, partners. Nor did he begrudge Tucker's desire to sit behind a desk – his buddy's short legs didn't allow him to run fast, anyway.

In Sam's view, he got the better part of the deal. Sam would play the Archie Goodwin detective, the one who schmoozes suspects by day and woos females on the dance floor by night. Sam didn't particularly care who solved the mystery. As the saying goes, poodles just wanna have fun.

In order to fulfill this life-long dream, our dynamic duo needed to convince a working detective to hire them. And to do that, they needed to be able to speak the language.

And so they practiced forming words like "perp," "lock 'em up," "dame," "fedora" and "pfui."

We won't discuss how long it took for the two friends to grow fluent in English. Suffice it to say that it was shorter than My Fair Lady but longer than "See spot run."

Once they could communicate clearly with the local children, they began answering Want Ads for private detectives.

That's when they discovered that not all humans are willing to recognize dogs as good orators. Time after time, they presented themselves at private investigating offices. Time after time, they were chased out with the words "I don't need no dang barking dogs!"

Barking. The detectives only heard barking.

Tucker and Sam returned to the streets. They talked to children in the local playground. The children talked back. Emboldened, they talked to the children's mothers. Many responded by pulling their children close and shrieking "get away!" A few, however, leaned forward and exclaimed, "You can talk!"

After a few days, the two friends realized that the problem wasn't in the way they enunciated their words. The problem lay in the human ability to listen. Most humans heard only what they wanted to hear. They weren't receptive to new ideas and thoughts.

Talking dogs was a concept most people couldn't – or wouldn't – accept.

Dachshunds, however, are known for their persistence. Poodles are eternally optimistic. The pair decided to soldier on until they found a private investigator willing to listen to what they had to say.

Leaving the "help wanted" ads behind, they pulled out the Yellow Pages, looked up "private investigators" and, starting at the top of the alphabet, began visiting offices.

One sunny day, they climbed the stairs of a seedy office building and found the door for Detective Bill O'Brian. By this time – having exhausted the A thru N part of the alphabet –

they knew polite knocking would not gain them entrance. It was far too easy for someone to slam the door in their face before they had a chance to say a word.

Sam stood on his hind legs and used his front paws to turn the door knob. Tucker pushed the door open. The two dogs entered a small office and paused to look around.

A battered wooden desk, its surface littered with paper, dominated the small room. Behind it, a rolling leather chair sat empty. A private investigator's license, framed, hung on the wall above the chair.

To the left, a dirty window looked out over the street. A small bookcase shared the right wall with a hanging Mickey Mouse clock and a door.

A toilet flushed, water shooshed then stopped and the door opened.

A stocky, overweight man wearing jeans and a flannel shirt stepped into the room. He was still looking down at the paper towel he was using to dry his hands, giving the dogs a chance to size him up.

He was tall, maybe just shy of six feet. His head was mostly bald, the hair having migrated to his cheeks and chin. What they could see of his lips were pressed into a thin line.

He crumpled the towel into ball, raised his head to focus on a metal trash can and lobbed the towel ball in that direction. The towel hit the rim of the can and fell to the floor.

The man scowled.

Sam trotted over to the paper, picked it up and – resisting the urge to shred it (most poodles have what's fondly called the "paper shredding gene") – and deposited it into the can.

By the time he returned to Tucker's side, Detective Bill O'Brian was gawking at them.

"How'd you get in here?" O'Brian's voice was three-pack-a-day rough.

"We're here about a job," Sam said. "We come as a set."

"You… you talk!"

"Finally!" Tucker sat down. "A detective who listens!"

"Yeah, well, you listen." The detective folded his arms. "Dogs don't work in this business. Believe me, I've tried.

"Criminals can spot German Shepherds, Doberman Pinschers and Rottweilers a mile away. Terriers want to be in charge. Golden Retrievers want to be everyone's friend. Bulldogs don't have the physical stamina, Beagles can't chase a perp without baying and Labrador Retrievers are easily distracted."

"We're not like any of those breeds," the dachshund said. "I'm Tucker and the big guy here is Sam."

Detective Bill eyed the odd couple. The

poodle was tall, so tall that his head reached Bill's belt buckle. His black, curly hair was tastefully cut short to the body, though someone had left boot-like poufs on his legs and fluffed his head, ears and tail.

The dachshund's long, silky hair was mostly black. Tan markings around the face resembled a Doberman's. At only nine inches tall, he looked totally ridiculous sitting next to the long-legged poodle.

"Just give us a moment to tell you why you need us," Sam the poodle said.

Bill crossed to his chair, leaned back and plunked his boots onto his desk.

"Okay, explain to me why I should hire not one, but two frou-frou dogs."

A low rumble sounded from the dachshund's huge chest. The poodle gently touched Tucker's shoulder, then returned his paw to the carpet.

"Our skills are exactly what you need," Sam said. "Tucker here can infiltrate even the smallest spaces. He can sneak around undetected, open zippers and track at ground level. He's even capable of rearranging the furniture to build a bridge to, er, items above his head."

He grinned. "With me around, of course, he seldom has to resort to such measures.

"I, on the other hand, can identify scents on the breeze, run faster than any criminal, pick pockets and, of course, also open zippers. You couldn't ask for a better team."

Bill studied the two dogs. They stared back with intelligent, alert expressions.

Intelligent, indeed. These two could talk! Even so…

Plunking his feet to the floor, Bill turned to his computer, pulled up a search engine and searched for dachshund character traits.

"Says here that dachshunds are always hunting for food," he said.

"I know the difference between the smell of a steak and a person," Tucker grumbled.

Bill typed in another search. "And here it says that poodles can be clowns and without provocation will start running in large circles."

"The technical term is 'zoomies,'" Sam said. "As Tucker said, we know the difference between work and play."

Bill frowned, thinking. If he hired these two, his fellow detectives would laugh. And laugh and laugh.

The bad guys would also laugh.

But maybe that was the point. While the bad guys were laughing, Bill would be catching them.

Besides, frou-frou dogs always attracted women.

"Okay, let's try it for a week," Bill said. "But you let me do the talking. If you're as good as you say, you've got a job."

The job was even more exciting than the two friends imagined. They used their excellent scenting capabilities to trail suspects from a distance and to see through people's attempts at disguise. They collected evidence without a warranty by removing it from suspects' pockets and purses and leaving it in plain sight. They even directed a wild car chase through city streets by hanging their heads from the window and following the villain's scent.

They weren't quite Nero Wolfe and Archie Goodwin. But they were happy.

There was just one problem: Bill.

While the detective was good at helping other people, he wasn't so good at taking care of himself. He smoked cigarettes and cigars, dined on French-fries and hamburgers and, aside from following someone on foot, seldom exercised.

By and by, the detective had a heart attack and landed in the hospital. The doctors told him he couldn't go back to work for a long, long time.

Which meant Sam and Tucker were suddenly unemployed.

"Grandpa, you can't do that!" Kim sat up in bed and folded her arms. "You can't take away

Sam and Tucker's favorite job!"

Max smiled and tugged his granddaughter's ponytail. "Who said I was going to take away their job?"

"But how can they be detectives without Bill?"

"That's what we're going to find out when I continue the story. Any other questions?"

"Yeah." Kim's eyes widened. "Do you think I could understand Sam and Tucker?"

"Of course." Max smiled. "You can understand anyone if you're willing to listen. Really listen.

"Now are you ready to listen to the story?"

Kim giggled.

"Yes."

After learning about their human partner's plight, Sam and Tucker considered their options.

The most obvious solution would be to accept a more traditional dog job and wait for Bill to recover. But after months of detecting, other jobs sounded dull, dull, dull.

"I don't want to herd some stupid sheep or guard a dark warehouse," Tucker said.

"So why don't we stay right here and remain detectives?" Sam suggested. "Bill's already advertised the business. All we have to do is wait for the customers to walk through the door, interview them and solve their problems."

The thought of actually fulfilling their dream of becoming Nero Wolfe and Archie Goodwin thrilled them. They moved their dog beds, toys, food and water into Bill's office and waited for customers.

The customers did, indeed, come. Most, however, couldn't understand what the dogs were saying and made a hasty retreat. The few who did understand stuck their noses into the air and stomped away.

After several weeks, the dogs remained unemployed.

"Maybe we should report them," Tucker said. "Isn't there some law against discrimination?"

"Don't think that covers us," Sam said.

Actually, what he said was "on't ink at o'ers us." Sam was practicing his pickpocketing skills and his front teeth were firmly clamped on the wallet that he was pulling from a coat Bill had left hanging on the coat rack. This, of course, made it impossible for Sam to pronounce the hard consonants.

After successfully removing the wallet without a single sway of the coat, Sam lifted a backpack and carried it to Tucker.

"Why don't you practice opening zippers?" he said. "We need to maintain our skills."

Tucker opened his mouth to remind Sam that the dachshund had taught this particular behavior to the poodle. But no words escaped because the door opened and SHE walked in.

Tall, blond, legs up to there, wearing a dead animal. She was class, real class, the kind that made males of all species stand up and pay attention.

Sam straightened. Tucker – who'd been sitting on Bill's leather desk chair – placed his front feet on the desk to get a better look.

The blond surveyed the office, her blue eyes moving from the coat hanging on the stand, to the window with the dusty panes, to the Mickey Mouse clock on the wall and finally, to the dachshund behind the desk.

Her face broke into a broad smile.

"Oh, you're so cute!"

Knowing how much Tucker hated being called "cute," Sam tossed him a warning glance before sidling over and leaning against the blond's leg.

"Well, hello handsome." She stroked Sam's head, then glanced around.

"Ah, hello?" she called. "Detective O'Brian?"

Tucker cleared his throat. This was the make-or-break moment.

"Bill isn't here right now," he said. "Sam and I are handling the agency while Bill recovers from an, er, injury."

The woman's eyes widened.

"You talk!"

"Yes, ma'am," Sam said. "I'm Sam and he's Tucker. We've actually solved most of Bill's cases."

"Talking dogs," the woman murmured. "Maybe that's just what I need."

Both dogs stiffened to attention.

"I assume you can talk to other dogs?" the woman said.

"Of course." Sam glanced at Tucker, then met the woman's eyes. "Not all humans understand us, though, so if your job requires interviewing those kinds of humans…"

The woman smiled. "Actually, I'd prefer that certain humans not understand you."

"In that case," Sam said. "Won't you please have a seat?"

While Sam led the new client to a chair, Tucker hopped onto the desktop and crossed over to them. This way he could look the woman in the eyes

She held out her hand. "I'm Angie Murgatroid."

After Sam shook her hand, she extended it to Tucker.

"So how can we help you, Ms Murgatroid?" Sam said.

"Please, call me Angie." She breathed deeply and for a moment tears formed in her blue eyes. "I need help finding my Afghan."

"You lost a blanket?" Tucker said.

"I believe our client is talking about an Afghan Hound," Sam said. "Tall, elegant, scored lowest on the dog IQ chart."

"Oh, but Benji is smart," Angie said. "I mean, for an Afghan. He knows his name and everything."

Sam and Tucker exchanged glances. They'd heard people often selected dogs that looked like them. Did Angie choose a dog who wouldn't be smarter than her?

Tucker reminded himself that Angie's neuron capacity wasn't the issue. She was a paying customer. If they handled this case correctly, no one would ever again hesitate to hire them.

"So," Tucker said, "when did, er, Benji go missing?"

"Two days ago." Angie pulled a monogrammed handkerchief from her purse and dabbed at her eyes. "We were at a local dog show. Benji was the favorite to win Best in Show. He easily won the Best of Breed."

She sniffed. "But when Charles – that's Benji's handler -- went to get him for the Group judging, he wasn't there. His crate was wide open and Benji was gone."

"Please excuse my ignorance," Sam said, "but where was Benji's crate?"

"In the handler's area, along with the other dogs Charles was showing. If you're thinking

Charles did something irresponsible, you're wrong. All of the handlers keep their dogs in their assigned space."

"So who had access to Benji's area?" Tucker said.

Angie shrugged. "Charles, of course. And his assistant. And, I suppose, anyone walking by the grooming area. The area is nothing more than one big room. The groomers use their tables, hairdryers, dog crates and other things to section off their space. People can easily wander in and out."

"Isn't someone always with the dogs?" Sam said.

"Charles' assistant is usually around. Sometimes, though, they get behind schedule and the assistant needs to bring the next dog to Charles.

"But even if no one was working in Charles' area, there are others nearby getting their dogs ready for the ring. You'd have to be pretty bold to waltz into the grooming area and steal a dog."

"Not if you were someone people expected to be there," Sam said.

"You mean Charles' assistant?"

"Or another handler or a judge or a ring steward."

"But why?" Tucker said. "Why would someone steal Benji? Have you received a ransom note?"

Angie shook her head. "No note."

"Revenge is always a good motive," Tucker said. "Does anyone hold a grudge against you?"

"Absolutely not. Everyone loves me. And Benji." She leaned forward. "I'm afraid that someone intends to show Benji this weekend as their own dog."

"How could someone do that?" Sam said. "Don't all show dogs have microchips? Even Tucker and I have them."

Tucker thought microchips were one of the greatest things invented. The tiny, computer-like chips allowed humans to easily locate their "lost dogs."

Dogs, of course, are never really "lost." They know exactly where they are.

But in Tucker's experience, humans want to control everything. This desire led to the invention of the microchip.

If a dog decided to visit his neighbors and was dumb enough to get caught by Animal Control, someone at the animal shelter would scan between the dog's shoulder blades for a microchip. The chip would identify the dog's human, a call would be made and the dog returned home.

Microchips were essentially a dog's get-out-of-jail-free card.

"Benji has a microchip," Angie said, "and I assume the other dogs do, too. But no one stands at the ring entry and scans the microchips of every dog who enters."

"So you're thinking someone intends to show Benji, win the competition… And then what?"

"Sell him." Once again Angie dabbed at her eyes. "Sell him for thousands and thousands of dollars. And I'll never see my Benji again!"

Sam, who wilted at the sight of tears, laid his head on Angie's lap, trying to offer comfort.

Tucker, however, had no tolerance for tears.

"If you've already given up," he said, "why hire us?"

Sam lifted his head and glared at Tucker. But Tucker was unrepentant; sometimes the only way to stop female hysterics was to shock them.

Sure enough, Angie's tears dried and she straightened her shoulders.

"I'm told that dogs can smell things that humans can't," she said. "That you can smell cancer on someone's breath, find a cadaver in sixty feet of water and track a week-old trail left by a specific human. Is this true?"

Though she'd addressed the question to Tucker, the dachshund was so astounded by the depth of Angie's knowledge – and that she knew the word cadaver – that he couldn't speak. So it was Sam who answered.

"All of that is true," Sam said. "Our noses

are more than a hundred times more sensitive that human noses."

He lifted his face. "We even have wing-like extensions on our noses. Can you see them?"

"Oh!" Angie studied Sam's nose. "I never noticed. Does Benji's nose also have wings?"

"Er, yes. Now watch what I can do." Sam twitched his nose.

"Oh, that's so cute! It's almost like that old television show, Bewitched, you know the one where the wife – she's a witch – twitches her nose to make rooms clean themselves or make a stain disappear or — "

Tucker couldn't take any more.

"There's nothing cute about it," he interrupted. "Our noses are serious tools. Rotating the sides of my nose helps me locate a specific scent."

"Then I've come to the right place." Angie looked from one dog to the other. "I want you to find Benji by going undercover at this weekend's dog show."

Sam's tail drooped. Tucker ground his teeth in frustration.

Dog shows. Why did it have to be a dog show?

They'd tried once to enter the dog beauty pageants and had been highly insulted. They'd stood while a so-called judge walked around them, then ran his hands all over their bodies. He even looked at their teeth!

He'd instructed them to move around the room.

Only then did he pronounce Sam "show quality." However, Sam wouldn't be allowed to enter a ring until he grew his hair into a lion's mane.

Sam was not pleased.

The judge missed Sam's reaction because he was now telling Tucker that the dachshund was definitely NOT "show quality." His bones were too large, his chest too broad, the hair on his feet too long.

Tucker's response cannot be duplicated in a bedtime story.

Unfortunately, the friends' bad experience with dog shows hadn't ended with their beauty pageant rejection.

A few weeks before his heart attack, Detective Bill decided to treat his two new partners to a fun day at a dog show. They'd planned to stroll the grounds, inhaling all the wonderful smells. They'd watch a few competitions, giggle at the poodle haircuts and the skinny dachshunds, buy hotdogs and soft-serve ice cream for lunch.

But when they'd arrived at the fairgrounds, the attendant wouldn't let them in.

He told Bill that only dogs who were entered in the competition were allowed. Sam wasn't wearing a show coat. Tucker was larger than the weight limit. Not entered, no admittance.

Bill had taken them to a park, instead, and later produced the promised hot dogs and ice cream. But they'd never had the opportunity to enjoy the aroma of hundreds of different dog breeds gathered in a single place.

"We would love to search for Benji at the show," Sam said. "But the organizers bar dogs who aren't entered in the competition."

Angie clapped her hands together. "I've already solved that problem. In addition to conformation, this show also includes an agility competition!"

Sam's eyes lit up. Tucker resisted the urge to crawl under the desk.

Agility, a canine obstacle course, required dogs to run through tunnels, weave through vertical poles, race across narrow planks and climb towering A-frames. The fastest dog wins.

Tucker didn't do fast. Nor did Nero Wolfe.

Tucker cast about for a way to refuse this case. Or at least avoid the agility course.

People tend to underestimate dachshunds' intelligence. This is because, compared, say to poodles or Labradors or golden retrievers, dachshunds aren't as concerned about pleasing their humans. Dachshunds, like terriers and other hounds, would rather please themselves.

In this instance, pleasing himself meant not running. When Tucker focused on a problem involving self-interest, he usually found a solution. It only took him a few seconds to find the perfect dodge.

"This all sounds lovely," he said. "But agility competitions require a human to run with the dog. And since the kidnapper will be suspicious if YOU suddenly entered agility. . ."

He let the sentence drift off, giving Angie the opportunity to find another way for them to go undercover.

Angie grinned.

"But I've got someone to go into the ring with you!" she said. "You'll be working with my niece, Kimberley."

"That's me!" Kim popped up in bed. "So I'm going to go undercover, too?"

Max grinned.

"Absolutely," he said. "Of course, you'll be a bit older in the story. The rules require that you must be at least ten years old to enter."

Kim nodded solemnly. But a glimmer in her eyes told Max his granddaughter wasn't ready to accept a "you're too young" rule.

Knowing Kim's penchant for finding ways around such rules, he hastened to resume the story.

"Before going undercover, Sam and Tucker had to meet Kimberley and learn all the rules…"

Angie drove Tucker and Sam to her niece's house, a small, one-story affair with a large fenced-in back yard.

As they opened the car doors, Kimberley trotted around the side of the house.

Dressed in the traditional childhood uniform of t-shirt and scruffy jeans, Kim's messy ponytail, horn-rimmed glasses and holes at her knees gave her an elfin appeal.

Even so, she was still a kid. Both dogs braced themselves for the typical child greeting: A sudden rush followed by grape-jelly-covered fingers wrapping around their shoulders.

Tucker slipped between Sam's legs, figuring he'd let the big guy take the brunt of the enthusiasm. To his surprise, Kim stopped a respectable distance away and extended her hand to shake their paws. She then reached into her pockets, removed what smelled like liver treats and offered one to each of them.

"If you need anything," Angie said, "I'll be in the house with your mother."

"We'll be fine," Kim said.

Tucker sniffed the air. There were more treats in Kim's pockets. Liver treats? He'd follow this kid anywhere.

He trotted merrily beside her, pushing Sam

to the outside so the big poodle wouldn't block the aroma of treats. They rounded the house and entered the backyard through a metal gate. A bunch of odd-looking stuff littered the area.

"This is all agility equipment," Kim said. "Today I'm going to show you the best ways to get on and off of the various obstacles without injuring yourselves."

She pointed to a variety of stand-alone fences. "Those are jumps. The height will be raised for tall dogs, lowered for shorter dogs.

"Over there—" She pointed to a series of vertical poles spaced evenly apart— "are the weave poles. Obviously, you have to weave through them. The trick will be to not miss a pole or you lose points."

"What about the treats?" Tucker asked

Kim grinned. "Those are to reward you when you do something right."

Tucker turned to Sam to share a paw bump. Sam, however, was staring wide-eyed at a contraption that looked a little like a bridge made of narrow planks.

Sam pointed at it. "What's that?"

"It's called a dog walk," Kim said. "You get on it here, walk up and across the top and down the other side."

Sam's eyes widened. "How tall is that thing?"

"It's only four feet high."

"They use wider boards for the big dogs,

right?"

"No. The width is the same for everyone."

Sam plunked his butt onto the round. "That's not fair. To cross that thing, the little dogs won't have to change the way they move their legs, but we big guys are going to have to step with one foot in front of the other."

Kim nodded. "I hear ya. But you big dogs will have the advantage when it comes to the A-frame."

She pointed to an A-shaped wooden mountain. Tucker's mouth went dry. "What are we supposed to do with that?"

"Climb."

"Climb? You mean with ropes and spikes and things?"

Kim laughed. "No, silly, you'll just run up it. Why don't we just get started? You'll understand this better when you try everything. I've set the jumps for the shorter dogs, so Tucker, you go first."

While Sam found a place in the shade, Kim led Tucker to what she called the "start line."

"I'm going to be yelling and pointing to the object you need to do first," she said. "So don't start until I shout the name of an obstacle. Ready?"

She pointed to a tire suspended between two poles.

"Jump!"

Tucker hopped through the tire and turned

to follow Kim. That's when he spotted the vinyl tunnel.

Now tunnels he understood. After all, Tucker's ancestors used to follow badgers into their tunnels and pull them back out by their tails. He ran into the tunnel.

"No, no, no!" Kim scolded. "You're not supposed to do that until I point at it."

"Does this mean I don't get a treat?"

Instead of answering, she led Tucker back to the starting line.

Kim guided Tucker through the weave poles with treats. The see-saw thingie – Kim called it a "teeter" – made an interesting thump when he crossed it. The dog walk seemed plenty wide, though Tucker made sure he didn't look down.

The very best obstacle, however, was the pause table. It took some effort to climb onto it, but once there, Tucker was allowed to sit while Kim counted down ten seconds.

Oh, the joy of sitting! The sun beat down, warming the rubbery surface. What a perfect place to lay down and snooze…

"Tucker! We're not finished yet. You're only supposed to wait here for ten seconds."

Tucker opened an eye. Kim waved a liver treat.

With a sigh, Tucker accepted the treat and hopped off the table.

Kim led him to the mountain.

Tucker stood at the base of the man-made cliff, wondering what numbskull designed it. Who could expect a nine-inch-tall dog to climb this thing?

"It's okay, Tucker, I'll help you," Kim said.

He rolled his eyes toward Kim.

"Er, sometimes it's easier to take a run at it," she said. "Just make sure one of your paws touches the yellow part here at the bottom."

The "yellow part" was a painted area that crawled maybe two feet up the side of the mountain. How could a dachshund possibly climb this thing without touching the yellow paint?

He backed away from the cliff, took a few deep breaths, then ran toward it. His feet hit the bottom of the frame and he scrambled upwards. Up, up...

Halfway to the top he lost momentum and began sliding backwards.

Kim reached out to grab him and hold him in position.

"If I support you, can you move one of your front paws?" she said.

Tucker gritted his teeth and reached forward with his right paw. Planting it on the cliff, he tried to drag a back foot after.

"That's good," Kim cooed. "Try pushing with your back legs."

"You have noticed that there's not much leg back there, right?"

"C'mon, Tucker, you can do it. Here, try to reach this."

She held a treat three inches beyond the dachshund's nose. Tucker's eyes brightened and he stretched forward and snagged the treat.

"How did you do that without moving your feet?"

Somewhere nearby, Sam snickered.

"How about I give him a push?" Sam said.

Kim shook her head. "No, the judges won't allow that."

Tucker's leg muscles, unused to all the activity, started trembling. Kim scooped him off of the A-frame.

"It's okay," she crooned as she found his favorite spot to scratch. "You've worked hard today. We'll try again tomorrow."

She set him onto the ground and held out an entire handful of treats. Maybe agility wasn't so bad after all.

As Tucker chewed, Kim turned to Sam.

"Okay, your turn."

Naturally, Sam sailed over all of the jumps, his floppy ears flying. He had to crouch to run through the tunnel, but he somehow managed without slowing much. Kim pointed toward the A-frame. Sam charged up, flew over the top and raced down the other side, somehow remembering to "put one paw on the yellow spot."

Kim was grinning from ear to ear. She pointed to the pause table.

Sam jumped over it.

"No, no, no! Weren't you watching Tucker? You're supposed to jump onto this and sit for ten seconds."

"Why?"

"Because that's the rules."

Sighing, Sam hopped onto the table, plunked his butt down and waited while Kim counted down.

She'd barely reached the "go" mark before Sam leaped from the table and over the next jump.

And then they came to the dog-walk.

Sam screeched to a halt.

"Are you sure big dogs use this thing?"

"Absolutely. Just put one foot in front of the other and you'll be fine."

Sam frowned, but started up the angled plank. He seemed to be doing fine.

Until he reached the top.

"Whoa, that's a long way down," he said.

"Don't be silly," Kim said. "You've jumped higher than this."

"Yeah, but that was jumping. This is walking the plank. Like on a pirate ship."

"Don't look down," Tucker said. "Just look at the board and put one foot in front of the other."

Sam nodded and reached forward with his

right paw. A back paw followed and, slowly, step by step, he started across the plank. When he reached the middle, however, he felt the plank bounce.

He froze. "What was that?"

"Did you feel a bounce? Don't worry, that's normal."

"Normal? Normal??? You expect me to keep my balance on a narrow, moving plank?"

"It was only a small bounce."

"I never felt it bounce," Tucker said.

Sam glared in his direction.

"It's not going to fall apart or anything," Kim said. "Keep going. You're almost there."

"I can't move," Sam said.

"Just one foot. See if you can move one foot."

But Sam remained a poodle statue.

"Tucker? Could you go get Aunt Angie please?"

Kim's voice was calm, but Tucker could smell the burst of fear. Though Sam had jumped higher than four feet, his current position made it impossible for him to safely leap off of the dog walk. And if he fell...

Tucker turned and raced to the house.

Angie must have been looking out of a window, because the back door opened before Tucker reached it. He explained the situation. Angie ran into the backyard.

Having exhausted a year's worth of

running in less than a day, Tucker returned at a more leisurely pace.

He arrived in time to watch Angie and Kim position themselves on either side of Sam and take turns moving his feet. When Sam reached the part that pointed down, he took two steps, then leaped from the board.

Tucker trotted over.

"Hey," he said, raising a paw.

"Hey, yourself," Sam replied, lifting his own paw.

They paw-bumped, then turned to Kim. She emptied her pockets and rewarded them with treats.

"Let's take a break and get a drink," she said. "Mom's fixing lunch."

They spent the afternoon and the following day practicing listening to Angie while navigating the obstacle course. While both dogs improved, Sam refused to touch the dog walk and Tucker never reached the top of the A-frame.

"It's okay," Kim said Friday evening. "The idea isn't to win but to give us a cover to look for Benji. No one will be suspicious if each of you avoids a specific obstacle. I'll need to cue it, but just run around it and we'll move on."

She invited the dogs to spend the night, saying her mother was making steak for dinner.

Sam and Tucker went to sleep with full

tummies.

Early the next morning, Angie drove them to the dog show. The parking lot attendant carefully examined Kim's agility entry, even going so far as to make sure only the two dogs registered to compete were in the van. Satisfied, he waved them onto the gravel parking lot.

Most every available spot was filled with campers, vans and SUVs. Harried looking people loaded dog crates, hair dryers, grooming equipment and other show paraphernalia onto rolling carts. Car doors slammed, dogs barked, footsteps crunched on gravel.

And the smells! Dog smells, people smells, car smells all mingled together into a confusing stew.

"How are we going to find Benji in all of this?" Tucker whispered.

"We'll find him," Sam said quietly.

"Did you bring Benji's favorite toy?" he said louder.

Angie nodded and pulled out a stuffed hedgehog stored inside a plastic bag. Kim took it, opened the top and held it so Sam and Tucker could stick their noses in for a good whiff.

"Do you want me to bring this with us, or will you be able to remember Benji's scent?" Kim said.

"If you have room in your backpack, it wouldn't hurt to have it with us," Sam said. "We're already getting bombarded with dog smells."

"The Afghans aren't scheduled to show until after lunch," Angie said. "We'll have time to poke around the grooming areas."

We? We???

For a moment, Tucker was speechless. The woman hired them to go undercover. Now she wanted to blow their cover by tagging along? Sheesh, she had no more brains than her Afghan. Maybe even less than an afghan blanket.

Sam, always the diplomat, spoke first.

"If the kidnapper is here and sees you," he said, "he might take Benji and run. Let us do the job you hired us for."

"But what am I supposed to do while you search?" Angie's voice was almost a whine.

"Stay here out of sight and watch people," Kim suggested. "If you see anything suspicious, come find us."

Before Angie could protest, Kim picked up the dogs' leashes and headed toward the large buildings.

"We need to check in with the agility folks before starting our search," she said.

"I still don't understand why we can't divide up the agility equipment," Sam said. "Tucker can take the teeter, dog walk, tunnel and pause table. I'll run the A-frame, weave poles and all of the jumps. We'll be a cinch to win."

"They only allow one dog into the ring at a time," Kim said. "Besides our main purpose is to find Benji. With any luck, we won't be here long enough to enter the ring."

Sam suddenly slammed to a halt and lifted his nose.

"Benji's been here," he said.

A gust of wind swept through the parking lot. "I'm sorry; I lost the scent."

"Don't worry," Kim said. "If Benji's still here, we'll find him. Let me know if you catch another whiff."

She led them into a crowded metal building. Dogs barked, crowds cheered, agility competitors shouted directions. Someone's sneakered foot tromped the tip of Tucker's tail. Tucker jumped and whipped around to growl at the offender. Suddenly, he was airborne.

"I'm sorry, Tucker," Kim said, holding him close. "I should never have counted on certain clumsy people—" this was aimed at a nearby teenager – "to watch where they're putting their big feet."

Tucker resisted the urge to stick out his tongue at the teen with the big feet. He settled into Kim's arms and surveyed his surroundings. From this height, he could see two rings, separated by white fencing. Agility equipment dotted each ring. Bleachers lined two sides of the rings. The far side of the building appeared to be some sort of staging area.

The line at the registration table was long. Sam stood on his hind legs to get a better look at the dogs running in the agility rings.

"Wow, doesn't that look like fun?" he said.

Tucker didn't even bother looking. "Nope."

Kim shuffled forward, scowling.

"Look at all the border collies!" she said. "We don't stand a chance."

Sam dropped onto all fours.

"Did we ever have a chance?" he said. "Tuck and I will both receive heavy point deductions when we ignore the dog walk and A-frame."

"Well, this was going to be a surprise," Kim said, "but I entered you in a Jumpers class. No contact obstacles, just jumps and weave poles."

Sam's eyes lit up. The only thing he preferred to running and jumping was putting his front feet on people's shoulders.

However, he couldn't help feeling slighted by Kim's concern over border collies.

"And you think a border collie can beat me?" he said.

"Well…" Kim glanced at the nearby agility ring. A black and white border collie raced over jumps, through weave poles, across the dog walk, more jumps, up the A-frame. The dog seemed to fly.

"Don't those guys have any sheep to herd?" Sam grumbled.

Kim ruffled his topknot.

"My Grandpa always told me that it's not the winning that's important," Kim said, "it's how you play the game."

They took a step forward.

"Of course," she added, "I never understood what he meant."

Kim signed in, accepted her number and crossed to a poster showing the running order.

"Looks like we have an hour or so before we have to return here," she said.

They left the building and Kim set Tucker on the ground. The outside air was fresh and welcoming, the noise level more tolerable. Sam lifted his nose, then shook his head.

"Nothing."

"Let's head toward the building where they're grooming the dogs for conformation," Kim said. "If Benji's still here, that's where he'll be."

As they strolled through the crowd, Sam and Tucker sniffed the breeze.

Tucker froze.

"I've got something."

Kim glanced at Sam, who shook his head.

"I don't smell it," Sam said. "But dachshunds are good trackers and I trust Tucker."

"Okay, Tucker, lead on."

Tucker pulled them to the right, weaving through smelly feet and dog butts. The fragrance grew stronger and he felt his heart rate increase. Finally, the odor was overwhelming. He sat and gazed longingly upward.

"You found a hot dog stand?" Kim said.

"Yeah, isn't it wonderful? I'll take mine plain, please."

Sam snickered. Kim rolled her eyes, but stepped up to the counter to order. Several minutes later, they found an empty picnic table. While Sam and Kim settled onto the bench, Tucker jumped onto the table and waited for Kim to set his plate in front of him.

"We should have gotten French fries," Sam said.

"Too greasy," Kim said. "If we're going to eat fries, let's get them at a regular restaurant that sells steak fries."

Tucker firmly believed that you ate what was near. But, hey, Kim was buying so she got to choose.

Besides, maybe later they could talk her into springing for ice cream.

Sam and Tucker wolfed down their hot dogs and waited patiently for Kim to finish hers. As she wiped her fingers with a napkin, Sam suddenly stood and sniffed the air.

"Tuck, do you smell that?"

Tucker lifted his nose and searched beyond the tantalizing odors of hotdogs, French fries and potato chips.

At first, all he could detect was the distinct fragrance of butter and popcorn. But then, beneath that, something that smelled Benji-like.

"Yeah, I think I do. But you'll need to take the lead on this one."

Even though Tucker's stomach was technically full, there was no way he could walk past the other food vendors without becoming distracted.

Kim picked up the leashes and followed Sam back onto the main path.

The big poodle trotted confidently, only occasionally pausing to cast side to side for a stronger scent. He led them to yet another metal building.

"Good work, Sam," Kim said. "This is where the groomers and handlers are setting up for the show ring."

"We have to be careful now," Tucker said. "We don't want to tip off the kidnapper that someone is looking for him."

Sam nodded and moved to Kim's left side. "Let me guide you by voice rather than leading. That way we won't stand out from the others."

They plunged into the crowd.

Dog hair floated in the air. The roar of hairdryers drowned out conversations. Sam and Tucker held their breath as they passed by a group of shar peis – sheesh, that wrinkled skin could really trap odors!

"Kim," Sam said, "without being obvious, look to your right. Does that Afghan in the padlocked crate look like Benji?"

A black and white Afghan, scrunched into the far corner of a large metal crate, trembled so violently that the crate vibrated. Fear pheromones poured from his skin.

Whoever this dog was, he deserved freedom. But the padlock holding the door closed made escape impossible.

"Benji didn't have any black on him," Kim said. "And he was always smiling."

They continued moving, but at a slower pace.

"I also smell something chemical," Sam said. "Maybe ammonia? Or peroxide?"

"Of course!" Kim stopped. "The kidnapper dyed him."

Sam urged Kim forward.

"We need to question the Afghan," he said. "And get a close look at the padlock. Let's turn around and walk by again. Do you recognize the man standing near the Afghan?"

Kim glanced over at the grooming set up. In addition to the crate containing the Afghan, a second, smaller one stood near the back wall. A foot or so away stood a table, a stand hair dryer, stacks of towels, a stool and grooming box. The area was so small it was amazing that the burly man could move without tripping.

Right now he loomed over a Corgi.

"Whoa," Tucker said. "Is that a Corgi with a tail?"

"Oh, isn't he pretty!" Kim said. "I love that sable color."

"Folks, let's stay on topic, please," Sam said. "Do you recognize the man?"

"No. But I wouldn't necessarily. I'm not involved in Aunt Angie's dog business."

"Good," Sam said. "That gives me an idea. Tucker, while Kim and I draw the man's attention, go ask the Afghan his name. And see if those padlocks use combinations or keys.

"Kim, can you act interested in the Corgi?"

Kim grinned. "I see what you have in mind. Let's do this."

They strolled toward the area where the man worked. As they neared, Kim stopped.

"Is that a Corgi?" Kim asked the man.

The man turned quickly, his shoulders tightening. Seeing only a child, he forced a smile.

"So you recognize a Corgi?" he said. "Most people don't know this breed."

"Oh, but I've never seen one with a tail."

Tucker feared the child-like gush in Kim's voice would make the man suspicious. To his surprise, the man puffed out his chest and launched into a lecture about Cardigan Welsh

Corgis. Big dogs on short legs, the dogs had been bred to herd livestock.

While the man expounded on the joys of Corgi-hood, Tucker slipped under the table and approached the crated Afghan. The hound did, indeed, smell like Benji's toy. Or, at least he did beneath the overpowering chemical odor.

"Pssst. Your name Benji?"

"Who … who wants to know?"

Oh, good grief.

"Angie sent me."

"Angie!" Benji leaped to his feet.

"Shh, keep it down. You wanna alert your jailer?"

Benji's eyes flicked toward the grooming table.

"Is Angie okay?" Benji whispered. "She hasn't burned the house down or lost her car in the parking lot or left her keys in the refrigerator or anything?"

"Er, no."

Of course, Tucker had no idea what Angie had been doing since they'd left her in the parking lot. But this guy was nervous enough without confessing that they'd left his mistress alone.

"You've got to get me out of here," Benji said. "Angie can't do anything without my help."

"So how'd you end up here?"

Benji's ears drooped. "Greed. The guy offered me steak. He must have laced it with something because I fell unconscious and woke up in this crate smelling like a steel mill."

"He died your coat."

"Ewww." Benji looked at his paws. "He turned my lovely russet fur to BLACK?"

His voice carried across the room. The man stiffened and his shoulders began to turn toward them. Tucker shifted back, away from the crate.

Sam suddenly leaped up, placing his front feet on the grooming table.

"No!" The man loomed over Sam and for a moment Tucker feared for his buddy's safety.

Sam, however, can move fast. He disappeared behind Kim, who'd pushed her shoulders back and lifted her chin, four and a half feet of contained fury.

"Don't you hurt my dog!"

"Then keep him away from my dogs. If he screws up Pond Scum's coat, I'll sue your parents."

"Pond Scum?" Kim said. "Why would you name this handsome dog Pond Scum?"

"His real name's Monty," the man said. "But I've got to lock him up before a show to keep him out of the fish pond. And after all that work, I don't need your poodle messing Pond Scum's coat."

"I'm sorry, mister. I promise to keep a

better watch on Sam if you'll finish telling me about Pond Scum."

Kim's transformation from irate terrier to contrite spaniel was mind-blowing. Tucker made a note to ask her for lessons.

However, Sam's distraction would only work for a few minutes. Tucker turned back to Benji.

"Look, here's the plan," Tucker said. "I'd hoped to just open your crate, but with the padlock on we'll have to wait until the kidnapper brings you out for the show ring. Then—"

"Show ring?" Benji's voice dripped scorn. "You mustn't know anything about dog showing. Contestants need to be physically gorgeous, but we also need to prance around the ring as if we own it. No judge is going to award a blue ribbon to a dog who looks like he's been beaten."

He glared at the man. "Robert knows that."

"Robert? You know this guy?"

Benji snorted. "'course I know him. He's Angie's ex-partner. You don't think I'd take steak from a stranger, do you?"

Tucker gritted his teeth. When they'd questioned her, Angie had denied knowledge of someone with a grudge against her. She never mentioned an ex-partner.

"So if he's not planning to take you into the show ring, what's he gonna do? Angie hasn't received a ransom letter."

Or, maybe she had and lost it.

But Benji was shaking his head.

"Robert has plenty of money," he said. "He's out for revenge."

Benji started trembling again. "I'm afraid he's going to hurt Angie by hurting me."

🐩

"Noooo!" Kim jerked up in bed. "Grandpa, you can't let Robert hurt Benji."

Hearing the panic in Kim's voice, Max felt his mouth drop open. Nothing scared Kim. Even though she was only six years old, she readily recognized the difference between reality and fantasy. After all, this was the grandchild who watched Godzilla and King Kong movies and cheered for the monsters.

He leaned and over and stroked her hair.

"Benji won't get hurt," he said. "Remember, Sam and Tucker are on the job. Er, do you want me to stop?"

"No!" She leaned back against her pillow and tucked the blanket around her teddy bear.

"Mr. Bear was a little scared, but he's alright now."

Max nodded solemnly.

"Then let's see what happens."

Tucker hastened to reassure Benji that they would rescue him long before Robert could hurt him.

"You don't think a dye job isn't hurtful?" Benji said. "Angie will be so upset."

Tucker rolled his eyes.

"Where does, er, Robert keep the padlock key?"

"I don't know." Benji started shaking. "I don't know, I don't know, I don't know!"

"Hey, you, get away from that crate!"

"Tucker, duck!" Sam shouted.

Tucker lowered his head just as a big boot whizzed over him.

"Run!"

Tucker didn't need to be told twice. He zipped between Robert's feet and charged toward freedom. Something crashed behind him, but he didn't stop to see what fell.

He wove through the crowd, his leash streaming behind him.

"Tucker, wait!"

Glancing over his shoulder, he spotted Sam and Kim running toward him. There was no sign of Robert.

He stopped and opened his mouth to tell them what he'd learned. Without breaking stride, Kim scooped him into her arms and continued moving.

"You can tell us about it later," she said. "We need to get to the agility ring."

"Agility?"

Tucker tried to stretch his body into a dachshund outrage position, but found it impossible to do while someone was holding him.

He settled for a scathing tone.

"Do you know how far I've run today?"

"Yes, and you've been very brave, too." Kim turned into the agility building. "Don't worry. I'm going to tell them you're sick and can't run."

"Does this mean I won't get to do Jumpers?" Sam said.

"No, I'm only going to forfeit Tucker's run. But you'll need to do a regular agility course first; Jumpers isn't until later in the day."

As they approached the judge's table, Tucker drooped his head and tried to look sick. The steward barely looked at him. She found his number and scratched him from the list. Whew!

In five minutes, however, Sam was doomed to face the dreaded dog walk.

Kim carried Tucker to a ringside chair and set him down.

"Okay, we only have a few minutes. What did you find out?"

Tucker recounted everything Benji had told him, including Benji's fear that Robert had something evil planned.

"Benji didn't know where Robert keeps the key to the padlocks," Tucker concluded.

"While Kim distracted Robert, I asked Monty," Sam said.

"You could have blown our cover!"

Sam shook his head. "Robert would never understand us. I'm sure he thought we were just barking.

"Anyway, Monty said Robert keeps the key in his back pants pocket. I could try picking his pocket—"

"No, let's not take any chances with someone mean enough to try to kick Tucker," Kim said. "I have another idea. Do you know how to pick locks?"

"Er, Bill tried to teach us," Tucker said. "But, well, you need fingers and opposable thumbs and—"

"Perfect! When Sam and I come out of the ring, you can tell me how to do it."

Both dogs protested. They'd grown fond of Kim and didn't want to risk her getting injured or, worse, sent to jail.

She brushed their arguments aside, saying they could stand guard while she worked.

The ring steward called Kim's number. She led Sam into the ring.

"Remember," she said as she removed Sam's leash, "I have to cue the dog walk but you don't have to climb it."

Sam stared around at the ring. He counted ten jumps – yippee! The section of weave poles appeared twice as long as the ones in Kim's backyard. In a clear attempt to confuse the dogs, the organizers had set the tunnel underneath the A-Frame. He'd have to listen closely to Kim so he entered the correct obstacle. The dreaded dog walk loomed at the far end of the course.

The judge counted down and Kim suddenly pointed to her left and shouted "jump!"

Sam raced toward a series of three jumps, clearing them easily.

"Teeter!"

Sam veered right and charged the seesaw. He leaped on, careful to touch the yellow spot, paused in the middle to shift position and allow the far side of the teeter to drop to the ground, then raced down and over another jump.

And then they neared the dog walk.

As promised, Kim cued the obstacle. Sam raced around it, then headed for another series of jumps.

At this point, the cheering was so loud that he couldn't hear Kim's next cue. But she was pointing at a flat, low jump. Oh, wow, a broad jump!

He cleared the jump and grinned back at Kim.

"That's not a jump!" Kim shouted.

She pointed at the object he'd just cleared. "Box!"

The strain in her voice broke Sam's heart. She clearly needed cheering. And that meant: Zoomies!

Sam pushed off from his back legs, leaped into the air and zoomed around the pause box. He ran so fast he created his own wind tunnel. His ears flapped, his tail wagged, his paws barely touched the ground.

Once, twice, three times he circled the box. As he came around for a fourth try, he spotted Kim actually standing beside the box, her finger pointing straight down.

"Hey, Kim," he shouted. "Watch this!"

He adjusted his angle and charged toward the box.

"Slow down!" Kim said.

But Sam had other ideas. He leaped onto the box, planted his front feet and dropped to his butt.

The brake specialists at Chevrolet and Ford could learn much about "stopping on a dime" by talking with a poodle.

The judge started his countdown.

Kim and Sam exchanged grins before Kim moved away. When the countdown ended, she shouted "weave" and pointed at the vertical posts.

Sam left the box and weaved.

Another jump, then the tunnel (and those judges thought they could fool a poodle, huh!), two more jumps and back to the A-frame/tunnel combination. This time Kim cued "frame."

Sam leaped onto the base of the frame, his back left foot catching the top of the yellow bits. As he neared the top, he glanced to his left and —

Whoa! Look at all the people!

There were old people and young people and people wearing jeans and people wearing dress-up clothes and they were all smiling!

Oh, look! That little boy just waved.

Sam sat and politely waved back.

The view from the top of the A-frame was breathtaking. He could see all the way to the door they'd entered.

A giggle drew his attention back to the audience. Another child was waving.

Sam waved to her, and then to the little girl at the end of the bench and then to the boy sitting two rows above.

More laughter. This was great!

"Sam!"

He waved to the cute kid wearing a poodle t-shirt.

"Sam!"

Flailing arms drew his attention to the right. Kim dropped her hands to her hips and glared up at him.

"Get down here!"

Was that a cue? Sam searched his memory. No, she'd taught them frame and tunnel and weave and box and jump (a cue actually invented by the first poodles, along with leap and zoomie).

Get down here was not in his agility cue repertoire.

"Saaaaam!" Kim pointed to her right. "Jump!"

Oh, boy, another jump!

With a final polite wave to the crowd, Sam ran down the frame, being careful to touch the yellow at the bottom (Kim will be so proud), and charged toward the new jump.

One jump, two jumps, three jumps, run, run, run and they were over the finish line!

Sam trotted to Kim, stood and placed his front feet on her shoulders.

"Did you see?" he said. "I remembered to touch all of the yellow spots!"

Kim's mouth dropped open and, for a moment, she simply stared. But then she pulled him in for a real hug and laughed.

"You did good, Sam," she said.

The ring steward approached with the leash. As Kim slipped it over his head, she said, "I gotta say that if Robert gets suspicious and wonders if we really entered agility, he'll find plenty of people who'll remember us."

They left the ring, wished the next team

luck and joined Tucker in the audience.

"I could tell by the laughter that you invented your own course," Tucker said.

"It was great!" Sam sat beside his best buddy. "You need to try it."

"Er, maybe some other time."

"So, tell me, how do I pick the lock on Benji's crate?" Kim said.

Once again both dogs protested.

"Do you have any other suggestions for opening that crate?" Kim said.

"Detective Bill once used a bolt cutter on a lock," Sam said.

"I doubt we'd find a bolt cutter laying around." She folded her arms. "Besides, what's the difference between cutting a lock and picking it? You guys will have to stand guard one way or another."

The two dogs exchanged looks, then sighed.

"Okay," Tucker said. "You win. To pick a lock, you'll need something called a hair pin. One large and one small."

Kim straightened and surveyed the agility audience. Surely, someone in this crowd had hair pins to share. She just needed to find the right person…

There. In the second row. That woman looked around Aunt Angie's age. Dressed in a skirt and low heels, she wore her blond hair in a French twist.

Grandma once tried to pull Kim's hair into that style. It required every hair pin in the neighborhood.

Surely, this woman could spare a pin or two.

"Wait here," she told the dogs. "I'm going to get some pins."

She trotted over to the blond, put on her most pitiful face and pointed at the hair that had fallen from her ponytail.

"Mom told me to bring hair pins," Kim said, "but I forgot. Do you have a couple of spares I could borrow?"

"Of course, dear."

The woman pulled a small cosmetic pouch from her purse, unzipped it and pulled out several hair pins.

"I only need two, a big one and a little one," Kim said.

"Nonsense," the woman said. "Two pins will never hold all of that hair."

She whipped out a brush and pointed to an empty chair.

"Now sit here while I fix this."

The woman's "do it now" voice sounded eerily like her mother's. Geez, if you used that tone with a dachshund, he'd swish off in a huff.

Kim plunked into the chair and winced as the Good Samaritan brushed the knots from her hair.

"You have lovely hair," the woman said. "Would you like me to style it like mine?"

"Er, no, a ponytail will be just fine, thank you."

Kim felt her hair tugged into position.

"When you do this yourself," the woman said, "don't put the elastic snug against your scalp. I'm wrapping it an inch or two from your head. Now I'm dividing the hair into two sections and tugging so that the elastic slides closer to your head. This will give you a bit of softness around the face. All we have to do now is secure the short pieces."

Kim flinched as the woman inserted hair pins.

"There! What do you think?"

She handed Kim a hand mirror.

"Wow," Kim said. "An adult ponytail! Thank you so much."

She returned the mirror, thanked the woman again and returned to the dogs. Her head throbbed.

Picking up the leashes, she said, "Let's go. We'll hide near Benji's area until we see Robert take Pond Scum to the Corgi ring. That should give us plenty of time to open the padlock."

"Grandpa, can you teach me how to pick a lock?"

"Ah, you do know that it's illegal to pick someone's lock?" Max said.

"Then why is Kim doing it?"

Max mentally hit himself. In his efforts to create a gripping story, he'd ignored the very real potential of teaching Kim something he shouldn't.

"Well, in this case, Kim is rescuing a stolen dog and returning him to his owner." He peered at her over his glasses. "Kim would never pick a lock to steal or explore or…"

He ran out of reasons a child might pick a lock.

"That's okay, Grandpa, I would never pick a lock unless it was absolutely necessary. So can you show me?"

Absolutely necessary. What would constitute an emergency to a six-year-old? Or, worse, a teenager?

"Er, I really don't know how to pick locks."

"Oh. Okay, I'll look it up on the internet."

Max cringed. Kim's parents were going to kill him.

"Shall we return to the story?"

They found an out-of-the-way spot near another groomer where they could observe Robert without him seeing them. It wasn't long before the big man slipped a show leash over

Pond Scum's neck, lifted him from the table and turned toward the conformation building.

As they passed, Pond Scum slowed and sniffed the air. Tucker tensed. The Corgi must have recognized their scent.

Fortunately, Pond Scum used good sense and didn't look their way.

As soon as Robert and Pond Scum were out of sight, they slipped into Robert's grooming area.

"Kim!" Benji slammed against his crate and began barking.

"Shhh. We don't want to draw attention to ourselves."

Kim knelt by the crate, slipped a hand through the bars and stroked Benji's neck.

"Don't worry," she said. "We'll get you out of here.

"Sam, could you please stand guard while Tucker tells me how to do this?"

Sam nodded and trotted to the entrance of Robert's area. He sniffed the air. Satisfied that the big man was nowhere near, he turned sideways. This allowed him to watch Kim and Tucker while still remaining alert for the scent of Robert and Pond Scum.

"You said I needed a large and a regular pin." Kim pulled a standard bobby pin from her hair, then felt around until she found one of the large pins. She yanked that out.

"Now what?"

Tucker pointed at the larger pin.

"Bend that into a straight line. Good. Now take maybe half an inch from the end and bend that into an L shape."

Kim did as the dachshund instructed, then held the pin up for inspection. Tucker nodded, then pointed at the smaller pin.

"You need to bend that one into a half-square shape."

The second pin was much easier to bend.

"Now what?"

"Insert the short L-part of the larger pin into the bottom of the lock. Now turn the pin in the direction the lock should open."

Kim studied the lock configuration, then slipped the large pin in and turned it slightly.

"Hold that pin securely," Tucker said. "Take the small pin and slip it in and out quickly. You should feel the lock's guts letting loose."

Kim's eyes slid sideways. "Did Detective Bill really call it the 'lock's guts'?"

"I'm interpreting. He said it was important to hold the big pin in place while you jiggle the smaller one."

Kim held the large bobby pin steady and slipped the smaller one in and out.

"Nothing's happening."

"Try jiggling the small pin."

Kim jiggled the pin. It snapped in half.

She pulled the damaged pin from the lock

and tossed it onto the ground.

"Tucker, can you pull another pin from my hair?"

Tucker placed his front feet onto Kim's shoulder and snagged a pin with his teeth.

"Ouch. Pull the other way."

The pin pulled free.

"Now help me bend it."

While Kim held one arm of the pin, Tucker used his teeth to pull the second one into place.

"Thanks."

She pushed the pin into the lock.

"Hey, guys?" Sam called from the opening. "I'm getting a faint whiff of Robert and Pond Scum."

Tucker clenched his teeth.

"I'm going as fast as I can," Kim said. "Rats."

The second pin broke.

"Detective Bill sometimes held a match under the hair pins, then doused them in cold water to strengthen them."

"Well, given that we don't have fire —" Kim tossed the broken pin aside " — we have to use what we've got. How many more pins?"

Tucker climbed onto Kim's shoulder. "Just one."

He pulled it loose and handed it to Kim.

"They're getting closer," Sam called. He reared up on his hind legs. "I can see Robert. We only have a few minutes before he sees us."

Kim jiggled the small pin. Benji urged her on.

"I heard a click," Tucker said.

Kim's eyes widened. She yanked on the lock. It opened.

Quickly removing it, she tucked the lock into her pocket and swung the door open. Benji bounded out.

"Hey, what are you doing?"

Robert appeared at the entry. Sam growled. Tucker frantically looked around. They were trapped against the back wall. There was no place to run.

Sam bared his teeth.

"What, you think I'm going to be scared by a girl and a poodle?"

Robert swung a foot at Sam. Sam backed away, but tripped over Pond Scum's leash. Robert's fist reared back.

"Don't you hurt my dog!" Kim charged the big man.

He easily brushed her aside.

"Kim!" Tucker flew forward and grabbed Robert's pant leg.

"Hey!" Robert tried to shake him off. But dachshunds are known for their tenacity. Tucker clung to that pant leg as if his life depended on it.

"We'll never outrun him," Pond Scum said. "We need a better plan."

"I've got an idea," Sam said. "Can you two

guys keep him busy so I can reach his back pocket? Kim, I need you to stay near me."

Pond Scum snapped at Robert's leg. Tucker released the pant leg, allowing Pond Scum the chance to grab it. Fabric ripped. Robert roared. Corgi and dachshund worked together, dashing in, nipping, then backing away.

Sam sneaked toward Robert. He could see the top of the key ring jutting just above the man's back pocket. Sam moved closer, closer. He stretched his neck and gripped the key ring with his front teeth.

When picking pockets, normally Sam would take the time to ease the item away so the owner wouldn't feel it moving. This time, however, he wanted Robert to know he was being robbed.

Sam yanked the key ring so hard that the pocket tore. Robert's hand whipped around, slapping the now empty pocket.

Tucker suddenly understood Sam's plan. He signaled Pond Scum, then backed away from Robert. Pond Scum followed his cue.

With the frontal attack ending, Robert whirled around to face the big poodle. Sam jiggled the keys, silently willing the man to chase him.

"Give me that!"

Robert lunged. Sam ran around the grooming table.

"This ought to be good," Tucker said to

Pond Scum.

They joined Benji at the back wall and watched Robert chase Sam around the table. Once, twice, three times.

In the meantime, Kim sidled over to the open crate door.

As Sam rounded the table for the fourth time, he tossed the keys to Kim. She snagged them from the air, then hurled them into the crate.

"Hey!" Robert ran to the crate and dropped to his knees. He stretched his arm, trying to snag the keys.

They'd landed just out of his reach. Frustrated, he ducked his head and moved partway into the crate. Again, he reached out. His fingertips brushed the edge of the keyring.

Sam slammed against Robert's butt. The big man fell deeper into the crate. Tucker, Pond Scum and Benji dashed forward and nipped at Robert's feet. Robert scrambled forward, away from the flashing teeth. His feet entered the crate. Kim slammed the door shut and slapped the padlock on.

Robert rolled onto his side.

"Let me outta here!"

"When you find your keys, you can let yourself out," Kim said. "Which is more than Benji was able to do."

"I'll find you and sue!" Robert bellowed.

"No, you won't." The strange voice came

from the aisle behind them.

Kim and the four dogs turned toward the speaker. A crowd of people had gathered. The woman who'd spoken stepped forward.

It was the lady who'd given Kim the hairpins.

"I'm not sure I approve of the way you used my hairpins." She smiled at Kim, then glared down at Robert. "But I am glad someone finally put an end to Robert's reign of terror."

She waved a manicured hand to indicate the people behind her.

"We've reported you many times for abusing your dogs," she said. "But you've been able to buy your way out of trouble.

"This time, however, you tried to abuse a child. In front of witnesses. I don't know if you'll wind up in jail, but I do know you'll never be allowed into the show ring again."

Robert's shoulders slumped in defeat. He cast one last glare at the crowd. Then his cold eyes shifted to Kim.

Kim resisted the urge to step back. She felt the kind woman move closer.

"He can't hurt you," the woman said.

Kim grinned up at her.

"I guess he learned a valuable lesson," she said. "Never underestimate a girl and her poodle."

"Did ya hear that, Mr. Bear?" Kim said. "Girls and poodles are tough stuff."

Max grinned.

"Did you like the story?"

"Yeah, but what happened after?"

"Well, Robert was so embarrassed that he'd been outwitted by a girl and her poodle that he moved out of town, leaving both Pond Scum and Benji with Angie."

"Did Sam get to run Jumpers?"

Max smiled. "Yes. And he won, too. Happy?"

"Yes."

"Now how about getting some sleep? Santa won't come if you're awake."

"There is no Santa, is there, Grandpa?" Kim said.

Max's heart ached.

A soft hand caressed his.

"It's okay, Grandpa," Kim said. "I haven't believed in Santa since last year. None of my friends think he's real. But sometimes it's fun to pretend, you know?"

"Like when you pretend that Mr. Bear is real?"

"Sorta." She put her hands over the bear's ears. "I love Mr. Bear and all, but he's not like a poodle, you know?"

Max studied his granddaughter. From the

living room, a grandfather clock chimed 10, 11, 12 times. Christmas morning had arrived.

And there would be no puppy.

Maybe it was time for honesty.

"Sometimes people have to wait until they're all grown up before they can have what they want."

"Like a puppy?"

Max nodded. "Like a puppy. But if you're willing to pretend, maybe there's something we can do in the meantime."

He stood. "Grandma will want to say goodnight. I'll go get her, okay?"

He returned to his bedroom to find Irene sitting at her vanity.

"I think we need to change plans." He told her what he wanted to do.

Irene smiled and kissed him. "You always find the best solutions."

Max crossed to the bedroom closet and pulled down a package hidden on the top shelf. He removed the contents and reached for his wife's hand.

They found Kim sitting up in bed reading a picture book to Mr. Bear. When she saw them, she set the book aside and smiled.

"All set for bed?" Irene enveloped Kim and planted a kiss on her cheek.

Kim giggled then looked at her grandfather.

Max cleared his throat. "Since it's already

Christmas, your grandmother and I want to give you the present from us. Are you ready?"

"Yes!"

Slowly, he pulled the stuffed poodle puppy from behind his back. It looked so real that they'd decided to not wrap it. Instead, they'd adorned it with a big red bow.

Kim squealed and reached for the toy.

"Fluffy!" she cried, pulling it close. "Fluffy, you're here!'

Max and Irene exchanged looks. They hadn't known that Kim had already named her yet-to-appear puppy.

"Oh, Grandpa, Grandma, this is the best Christmas ever! Thank you, thank you, thank you."

She cuddled the toy to her chest.

"Now, you'd better get some sleep," Irene said. "You have a big day ahead of you. I'm making French toast for breakfast"

"Yippee!"

Irene leaned over and kissed her granddaughter. Turning, she winked at Max and left the room.

"Grandpa? Thank you for, you know, telling me the truth."

Max fought tears.

"You know," he said, "you might have to wait until you're all grown up to get a real puppy."

Kim nodded. "That's okay. Now I have

Fluffy."

She grinned. "But don't tell anyone I said that."

🐩

Did Kim ever get that poodle puppy? Did she learn to pick locks? Did a childhood of listening to Grandpa's tall tales have unexpected consequences? (You just know it did or I wouldn't have asked the question.)

Find the answers in the five-star mystery series that features a grown-up Kim and her jeweler grandfather.

Readers fall in love with the heart-warming cast of characters, savor the interwoven gemstone legends and lore and laugh at the antics of two precocious dogs.

Sound like fun? Please turn the page to read an excerpt from *The Blue Diamond*, the first in the Jeweler's Gemstone Mystery Series.

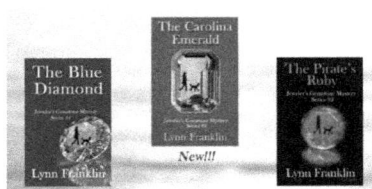

Warning: These books do not contain talking dogs.

The Blue Diamond

Jeweler's Gemstone Mystery #1

Prologue

**22 Years ago
Osprey Beach, Maryland**

"Grandpa, you lied to me!" Kimberley West stomped into the Osprey Beach Jewelry office with all the indignation an eight-year-old could muster.

Max Hershey looked up from the .78 carat diamond he was setting to find his favorite granddaughter glaring up at him. The Chesapeake Bay breezes had pulled strands of brown hair from her ponytail and she'd torn a hole in her new jeans. The flash in her brown eyes prevented him from kissing the dirt smudge on her freckled nose. The little hellion clutched her well-worn stuffed poodle in one arm, a heavy book in the other.

"What do you have there?"

Kim held out The Encyclopedia of Gemstones, the one he'd left sitting on the diamond display case.

"Pretty heavy reading for a little girl," he said, taking the book from her.

Hearing the amusement in his voice, Kim rolled her eyes. Why did adults always assume a kid couldn't use a dictionary? Besides, Grandpa was trying to change the subject.

"You lied," she repeated.

With a sigh, Grandpa removed the specially made glasses with the attached magnifiers and laid them in the center of the workbench. Donning his regular glasses, the ones with the lines across the bottom, he peered down at her.

"What makes you say I lied?"

"You said the colors in opals were made by butterfly wings."

"Uh, huh."

Kim pointed at the book. "It says in there that opal color comes from iron and carbon and mang . . . mang . . ."

"Manganese."

"Yeah."

Kim crossed her arms, Fluffy now forming a barrier between her and the man she'd always trusted.

Grandpa pulled Kim into his lap. It was large, soft and always, always safe. But today, Kim resisted the urge to snuggle against him. She sat rigidly, her sneaker clad feet swinging in the air.

"Didn't you like my stories?" Grandpa said.

Kim reluctantly agreed they were good stories.

"Weren't they more fun than talking about iron and carbon and manganese?"

"Not if they weren't true."

"Nancy Drew isn't true and you like those stories, don't you?"

"Yeah, but no one ever said Nancy Drew was real."

Grandpa sighed, his breath warm on her cheek. "Tell you what, if I promise to tell you when a story is true and when it isn't, will you forgive me?"

Kim's mouth twitched. "Maybe."

"How 'bout if I give you a present and tell you a true story?"

Giggling, Kim threw her arms around his neck. "Definitely."

She heard his chuckle as Grandpa eased her to the floor, then turned to reach into the center drawer of his workbench. Kim set Fluffy down; she needed two hands to accept a fist-sized chunk of golden-brown. The stone was smooth to the touch and emitted a warmth that made it feel alive. She could see through the stone, all the way to the center where a honeybee appeared to be flying in a cloud of gold.

"That's called amber," Grandpa said. "It came from the resin of ancient pine trees, resin that's hardened. The bee was trapped in the resin when it was still sticky. It's been sitting inside the amber for 50 million years waiting for a little girl to appreciate it."

Kim turned the silky stone in her hands. The bee was perfect, its fuzzy shoulders giving way to the gold and black bands just like real bees.

"Oh, Grandpa," she breathed. "It's perfect."

The bell to the store jingled. Grandpa glanced through the window that separated the office from the store front and stood.

"Come say hello to your Aunt Emerald," he said.

Kim grimaced. Aunt Emerald smelled like wet leaves and she treated Kim like a baby.

Grandpa sighed. "I might be able to find a piece of chocolate for a good girl . . ."

"Deal." Setting the amber carefully on Grandpa's desk, Kim lifted her poodle and tagged behind Grandpa into the store. Despite the summer heat, Aunt Emerald was wearing her bossy clothes: high heels, tight skirt and scratchy square-bottomed jacket. Kim wrinkled her nose as her aunt bent to offer a powdered cheek. Feeling Grandpa's fingers tighten on her shoulder, Kim quickly kissed the air near her aunt, then climbed onto a stool.

Aunt Emerald straightened and produced a small jewelry box from the purse Mom said cost as much as a car.

"I found these at an estate sale," Aunt Emerald said. "Are they diamonds?"

As Grandpa opened the box, Kim leaned forward to peer inside. But it contained nothing more than two clear stones set in what Grandpa called studs. Boring.

Grandpa slid the box in front of Kim. "Let's see if you remember your after-school lessons."

"For heaven's sake, Dad, just use that tester thing."

"Gemologists can't depend on gadgets, can they, Kimmy? Besides if the Russians perfect their diamond maker, that tester will be useless." Grandpa smiled down at Kim. "Go ahead, honey, let's see what you remember."

Kim's hand trembled as she removed one of the earrings from the box. The diamond lesson had been last week, but it seemed like long, long ago. He'd begun by telling her what he called "the old wives' tale" about diamond being the only gem that could scratch glass. Anything harder than glass, he'd said, -- even plain old quartz -- will scratch glass. And then he'd told her to . . . to . . .

She closed her eyes, trying to visualize Grandpa's lesson. She could see him standing beside her as he was now, holding a ring. He'd brought the ring towards his mouth and . . .

Opening her eyes, she breathed onto the earring. The gemstone fogged. One-one-thousand, two-one-thousand, three-one-thousand . . . The stone stayed foggy.

Diamonds didn't stay foggy. She smiled up at Grandpa. But before she could say anything, Grandpa placed a finger over her lip. "Remember, don't jump to conclusions. What happens next?"

"I, er, look at it through the . . . the . . ."

"Loupe. Remember?" Grandpa handed her the gadget that would make the gemstone look ten times bigger.

Aunt Emerald snorted. "I did all that. If I can't tell the difference, how do you expect a child to?"

Kim bit her tongue. Grandpa didn't like her sassing her aunts. Which wasn't fair 'cause they sure sassed her.

But Grandpa was doing his own sassing. "If you'd paid attention when you were Kim's age, you wouldn't be asking me to make the identification."

Kim held the . . . the loupe to her eye, just the way Grandpa showed her. She drew the earring towards the loupe until it came into clear view. Look at the edges, Grandpa had taught her. Diamond edges are always sharp. Diamond look-alikes have softer edges.

But without another stone to compare, Kim couldn't tell if these edges were sharp or soft. Looked pretty sharp to her.

She bit her lip and glanced at Grandpa. His smile calmed the butterflies in her stomach.

"Look deeper."

Deeper. Oh, yeah. Diamond look-alikes often had telltale flaws. Like . . . like . . .

"Bubbles!" Kim grinned at Grandpa. "I see bubbles!"

"Nonsense." Aunt Emerald snatched the earring and loupe from Kim's hand and bent to study the stone. With a snort, she looked up. "I see a tiny inclusion. Not a bubble."

Kim wrapped her arms around Fluffy and watched Grandpa bring the loupe and earring to his eye. A slow grin spread across his face.

"Kim's right; it's a bubble." Grandpa set the loupe on the counter and turned to Kim. "And a bubble means?"

"Glass!"

"Excellent." Grandpa turned back to Aunt Emerald. "Better get your contact lenses checked." He tucked the earring back into its case. "Hope you didn't pay diamond prices for these."

Aunt Emerald's nose wrinkled. "I know better than that. Only paid a dollar." She waved her hand over the box. "Maybe you can sell them to someone who doesn't give a sh . . . er, doesn't care."

"These are nice simulants. Sure you don't want them?"

"Absolutely not." Aunt Emerald scooped up her purse. "Tell Mom I couldn't stay; I've got a meeting in Annapolis."

She pecked Grandpa on the cheek, turned and swung the door wide, admitting the fragrance of an Osprey Beach summer: the Bay's brackish water, suntan lotion and sand.

Picking up the earrings, Kim followed Grandpa back into his office and grinned as he pulled a piece of brightly wrapped chocolate from his desk drawer. He handed it to her, touched her cheek, then settled into his chair.

Kim plopped onto the floor and admired the candy's bright blue foil. It was as pretty as anything in Grandpa's store. Grandpa said the candy was made in Switzerland, where he was born. Her mouth watered as she imagined the silky smoothness and deep chocolate flavor.

But . . . she'd peeked into Grandpa's drawer. This was the last piece. Did she really want to eat it now? It came all the way from New York, where Grandpa traveled to buy his gemstones and jewelry. And he wasn't scheduled to go back to New York until next week!

"Don't worry," Grandpa said, "I have more." He peered over his glasses. "Hidden."

Kim giggled. She popped the chocolate into her mouth and carefully refolded the pretty foil. Twirling the satiny dark chocolate around her tongue, she held the open earring box towards the overhead light and rotated it back and forth so the earrings caught the light. She glanced from the earrings to the diamond ring Grandpa held.

"Grandpa?"

"Hmmm?" Grandpa put on his expensive glasses and studied the ring.

"Why didn't Aunt Emerald want the earrings?"

"Because they're not real diamonds."

Kim touched the edge of an earring. "Did someone tell her a story that wasn't true?"

Grandpa chuckled. "No, your aunt makes up her own stories."

Kim looked again from the earrings to the ring. "But they look like diamonds. Aunt Emerald couldn't tell the difference. So why didn't she want them?"

Grandpa peered over his glasses at her. "Wouldn't you rather own something real than something fake?"

Kim shrugged. "Not if they're just as pretty."

"But . . ." Grandpa's eyes darted around the room, finally landing on Fluffy. "Wouldn't you rather have a real dog than a stuffed one?"

Kim giggled. "That's silly. Even a blind person can tell the difference between real and stuffed."

Grandpa stared at her, his expression unreadable. Finally, he reached out and tugged her ponytail.

"Let's be thankful other females aren't as pragmatic."

"What's prag . . pragma . ."

"Pragmatic. It means you have a logical way of looking at the world."

"Is that good?"

Grandpa blinked like something was in his eye. But then he reached out and stroked her cheek.

"Just as long as you can still enjoy my stories."

Chapter 1

Present Day
Crater of Diamonds, Arkansas

A loud buzzer shattered the still summer air. All heads turned towards the diamond field.

For a moment, everyone froze, noses lifted, bodies stiff, human setters on point. A second passed, two.

"Mommy, let's go!"

Tension broken, the diamond hunters bundled the remains of their lunch, gathered buckets, pails and screens and hurried towards the Diamond Discovery Center. Within minutes the picnic area was empty except for a pony-tailed woman and a black standard poodle.

Kim West pinched off a piece of hamburger and passed it to Rorschach.

"And that is what they mean by diamond fever."

Rory tilted his head in agreement. Or maybe he just wanted another bite of hamburger.

Kim pushed away her own half-eaten lunch, leaned against the picnic table and turned her face to the sun filtering through the overhead tree branches. After living five years in rainy Oregon, the hot Arkansas air felt glorious.

She wondered briefly if, now that she was moving back to Maryland, she'd tire of summer heat and humidity. Here the air was so heavy it carried the smell of wet dirt from the diamond field across the parking lot and into the picnic area. Kim suppressed a groan of pleasure. She couldn't wait to start digging, looking for amethyst, agate, jasper and quartz.

But not diamonds.

Despite the diamond fever that hung over the park, infiltrating even the youngest child's bloodstream, Kim was immune to diamonds.

Her cell phone announced itself with the theme from Indiana Jones. Kim pawed through her heavy shoulder bag . . . extra glasses, dog treats, wipes for Rory's feet, AAA guide, maps, flashlight, dog-training clicker . . . ah, cell phone. She smiled as she read caller ID and flipped the phone open.

"Hey, Grandpa!"

"Hello there, Monkey. How's your cross-country trip? You didn't try to climb one of those Redwood trees, did you?"

Kim giggled. "Their bottom branches were a little too high to reach. But Rory hiked his leg on one."

"Good for Rory." Only Grandpa, who'd read John Steinbeck's Travels with Charley, would understand the significance of a standard poodle recognizing a giant Redwood as a tree. Unlike Rory, Steinbeck's poodle showed no interest in the trees.

"Where are you now?"

"We just got to Crater of Diamonds . . ."

"Looking for diamonds?"

The excitement in Grandpa's voice made her ache. Poor Grandpa. He'd been so thrilled when she graduated with a degree in geology -- and so disappointed when she went back to school to study psychology. Despite the fact that her dissertation, How the Diamond Industry Brainwashes Women, landed her a coveted professorship, Grandpa still hoped she'd someday return to her roots. He didn't understand her fear that the family's diamond obsession would smother her. Or that she honestly, truly despised diamonds and all they stood for.

As much as she hated diamonds, however, she loved the grandfather who sold them.

Keeping her tone light, she answered "Just looking forward to getting dirty. Wish you were here."

Instead of the expected excuses -- he couldn't trust her aunts to watch the store and couldn't afford to close for a week -- she heard silence. No, not silence. A low hum like . . . traffic? In Osprey Beach?

"Grandpa, where are you?"

"New York."

"But you were in New York last week." Wasn't he? Had she lost track of time in the whirlwind of packing to move back to Maryland?

"Something came up."

Kim straightened and gripped the phone. "What's wrong?"

"Nothing's wrong," Grandpa said. "Just wanted to know how soon you'd be home."

But Kim knew every nuance in her grandfather's voice. The tightness suggested an attempt to suppress anger. Nothing unusual there; Grandpa's four daughters often tested his patience. What worried Kim was the high pitch and quiver.

Almost like he was afraid.

"Something's wrong. I know you too well."

Her own voice must have sounded odd.

Whining, Rory shoved something into her free hand -- an acorn he'd retrieved from the ground -- and leaned against her. She stroked his ear reassuringly.

Grandpa sighed. "I never could hide anything from you."

"Yeah, so don't start now. What's going on?"

"Probably nothing. A friend poked at a hornet's nest and I'm supposed to keep him from getting stung."

His voice was still tight with frustration, but the squeakiness was gone. Maybe she just imagined the fear.

Besides, Grandpa's friends were mostly old men whose idea of adventure was wrestling a rockfish into a boat. How much trouble could they get into?

"What can I do to help?" She passed a bite of hamburger to Rory and popped a fry into her own mouth.

"I could sure use another mind to work this through. Maybe put that psychology degree to use."

Kim couldn't help smiling. At long last, Grandpa acknowledged her degree as useful! He'd always dismissed her psychology studies as nothing more than "woo-woo."

"So tell me what's up."

"It's complicated."

"I'm a big girl now. I can handle complicated."

A long sigh. "I don't suppose I could postpone this conversation by enticing you with a new pair of earrings?"

"Nope."

"How 'bout chocolate?"

Kim tried to suppress a giggle. It came out as a snort.

"Seriously, Kim, this really needs to be discussed in person. How soon will you be home?"

There it was again, a tension totally alien to Grandpa's character.

She was, what, eighteen, nineteen hours from Osprey Beach? If she drove. If she flew, however . . . She could probably catch a plane in Little Rock. But that would require crating Rory in cargo. No, better to find a local kennel, fly to Maryland, then fly back to Arkansas to pick up Rory and her van.

"I could catch a plane, be there tonight."

"Thanks, sweetie, but that's not necessary."

Kim breathed out through her mouth. Good. She really didn't want to abandon Rory.

"Well, then, why don't I just drive straight home?"

"Don't cut your trip short. Just get here when you can."

Kim knew better than to argue. Always better to say nothing and do what she wanted.

She changed the subject to her cross-country trip, regaling Grandpa with stories of high desert, towering mountains and plunging canyons. As they chatted, she pictured Grandpa making his way through New York's Diamond District.

She'd been ten years old the first time Grandpa took her on a diamond buying trip, but she could still remember the thrill of stepping out of the taxi onto West 47th Street. The street itself was narrow, making its crowded sidewalks appear wider. Tourists dressed in shorts and t-shirts stood before awning-covered storefronts, gawking at the glittering displays of diamonds. Business-suited men and women clutched jewel-filled briefcases as they wove through the crowd. Hawkers called to passersby while Hasidic diamond buyers in long black coats slipped smoothly through the crowd. Having just read a mystery set in Egypt, Kim likened the scene to a Cairo bazaar.

Only later, as an adult, did she realize the similarities included danger. Pickpockets and would-be thieves haunted the sidewalks, waiting for couriers to exit diamond trading centers, stalking their prey, looking for an opportunity to pounce. In response, merchants hired more security guards. Strategically placed video cameras helped deter impulse snatch-and-runs. But the truly determined simply changed tactics, using disguises and machine guns to rob the stores themselves.

Grandpa, of course, usually dismissed Kim's concerns, saying no one would bother him. After all, who would guess his ratty old briefcase contained a fortune in gems?

Today, however . . . that was tension she heard in his voice.

She opened her mouth to push for an explanation, but Grandpa was already talking.

"Well, I'm here, they're waiting, drive carefully, love you." Click.

Kim frowned at the phone. That stinker! He knew she was going to push for more information. She punched in Grandpa's number on her speed dial. The phone went immediately to voice mail.

Sighing, she closed her phone. At 76, Grandpa could still outsmart her.

Rory stood, his tail wagging furiously. Kim looked across the parking lot, towards the diamond field. Some of the diamond hunters were returning.

Though crowded by Arkansas standards, the Crater of Diamonds park was worlds away from New York. No hawkers, no business suits, no shady looking characters. Just a bunch of sun-burned families covered in the diamond field's odd greenish colored dirt.

Next to her, a mother laid out Kentucky Fried Chicken while her son and daughter -- good heavens, they couldn't be more than five or six years old -- arranged a collection of stones.

Seeing Kim's interest, the mother flashed a weary smile. "Did you see the yellow diamond the little girl found? They said it's 10 points."

Ten points. The size of a match head.

Still the child who found it would long remember today, digging in the dirt, finding the stone, hearing the buzzer announcing a diamond find -- her diamond find -- watching the people crowd around to see what she'd discovered. Maybe she'd grow up to respect geology.

Or maybe she'd just become another diamond-crazed airhead.

Kim sighed and gazed longingly towards the plowed field. From this angle, however, she could see nothing but parking lot, trees and excited families entering the Diamond Discovery Center.

Grandpa should be here, darn it, not traipsing around New York with a battered briefcase full of jewels.

After all, the trip to Crater of Diamonds State Park had been Grandpa's idea. He'd talked about bringing her here ever since she was six years old and he caught her digging up his backyard looking for gemstones.

Instead of chastising her for messing up his rose garden, he'd taken her into the house, cleaned the dirt off her face and began teaching her the natural history of gemstones. He'd placed a piece of black coal in one of her hands and a glittering diamond in the other and explained how -- though they looked totally different -- they were composed of the exact same chemical element: carbon. Calling the diamond a miracle of nature, he'd snagged a jewelry catalog and sketched pictures to show how high pressure and extreme temperatures deep in the earth transformed carbon into the world's most precious gemstone.

Though she understood only half of his words, she'd grasped the idea that there were diamonds in Arkansas and some day she and Grandpa would hunt for them.

But the promised trip never occurred. As sole proprietor of Osprey Beach Jewelers, Grandpa was reluctant to leave his business in someone else's hands. Of his four daughters only one -- Kim's mother -- was dependable.

Mom, however, had her own job teaching high school English and, in any event, she'd never been able to control her three younger sisters. If Aunt Emerald, Sapphire and Ruby decided to use the store as a personal jewelry box, Mom would stand by helplessly. And Dad had more sense than to get involved.

This time Kim suggested Grandpa ask Aunt Ginny to watch the store. What Dad's older sister lacked in height, she more than made up for in attitude. She'd have no problem standing up to the other aunts. And now that Ginny had retired from the Motor Vehicle Administration, she was desperate for distractions.

Grandpa, however, was paranoid. Kim couldn't blame him, really; if she was sitting on all those diamonds, rubies and other gems, she probably would be, too. In the end, he'd refused Aunt Ginny's help and once again the promised trip fizzled. Kim set off across country, alone.

Dreams, however, never die easily. Despite Kim's aversion to all things diamond, she couldn't resist the opportunity to dig in the field that had captured her childhood imagination.

But not today. Today she needed to get on the road, drive as fast as she dared to reach Grandpa. He said he needed her.

And she couldn't shake the sense that when he called, he'd been truly frightened.

Chapter 2

Kim pushed the old minivan all day and through the night, thrumming tires keeping time with the chanting in her head: Grandpa needs me, Grandpa needs me, Grandpa . . . Her brain devised and dismissed scenarios that would make Grandpa afraid. Family illness. Lawsuit against the store. Robbery. But Grandpa wouldn't hesitate to reveal those over the phone. What would make him secretive?

Her brain whirred. The miles ticked away, the tedium interrupted only by ammonia-scented rest areas and machines stocked with stale crackers and expensive drinks. Grandpa needs me, Grandpa . . .

At noon on the second day, she pulled into a sun-scorched rest area just north of the Tennessee/Virginia border. Heat radiated from the asphalt parking lot and the moisture-laden air wrapped her bare shoulders and made it difficult to breathe. For the first time, she longed for Oregon's dry, low-heat summers.

While Rory sniffed a patch of brown grass, she dialed Grandpa's cell phone.

She pictured Grandpa puttering in the light-filled kitchen above the store, pouring iced tea or assembling one of the crazy sandwiches they'd invented together. As the phone rang, her mouth watered with the memory of peanut butter, banana and chocolate syrup sandwiches. She hadn't had one since she last visited Grandpa; it just didn't taste the same without him.

When Grandpa answered, however, the background clank of trucks running over manhole covers revealed a totally different location: Manhattan.

"You spent the night?" Grandpa never stayed in New York. Too expensive, too noisy, too unlike home.

A chuckle filled her ears. "And hello to you, too. Find any diamonds?"

"Actually, I just crossed into Virginia."

"I'm sorry; I didn't mean to cut your trip

short."

But she could hear the delight in his voice. "Don't worry; you now owe me a trip to Crater of Diamonds. Together. Like we planned."

Grandpa's musical laugh made her smile. Calling to Rory, she headed back to the van.

"So why are you still in New York?"

"Long story." There it was again; that back-of-the-throat rumble. Grandpa's worry voice.

Before she could quiz him, he added "When I get home I'll need your advice."

"Well, you know I always have opinions." Good, he laughed. "So how soon will you be home?"

"Train gets into Baltimore around seven, so unless traffic is bad, I should be there by eight."

Perfect. Her GPS estimated the final leg of her trip at eight hours.

Anxious now to get on the road, she wished him a safe trip, closed the phone and strapped Rory into his seatbelt.

"Wanna go see Grandpa?"

Rory responded with a lick and a grin.

Seven hours and fifty-four minutes later, the four-lane narrowed to two and the twilight gray water of the Chesapeake Bay came into view. Sensing the nearness of the water -- or maybe Kim's excitement -- Rory stood and snuffled at the back window. Kim cracked the windows and joined the big poodle in inhaling deeply.

Honeysuckle, fresh-mown grass and wet sand. The water itself, however, seemed odorless. So different from the wild, salty odors that emanated from the Pacific Ocean.

But she'd grown up near the Chesapeake Bay, splashed in its brackish water, explored its fossil-rich shores. The Pacific might trigger a deep sense of awe, but she preferred the soothing rhythms of life on the bay.

The speed limit dropped to thirty and the water loomed larger. A freighter chugged across the horizon, but the water just offshore showed nary a ripple. As she neared the intersection with Bayside Road, the street that paralleled the bay, the traffic light turned red.

Kim groaned. Since leaving the Virginia rest stop, she'd encountered an endless succession of red lights, construction gridlocks and kamikaze commuters. Now a steady stream of cars prevented right-turn-on-red. Where had all these people come from? Had the Three Beaches -- Osprey, North and Chesapeake -- changed that much in the two years since she'd last visited?

She squinted at a license plate. Virginia. And the one behind it was Pennsylvania and beyond that was Delaware and . . . Tourists. Why so many tourists . . .

"Yes!" Kim punched a fist in the air as she figured it out. "Do you know what next week is?" In the rear view mirror, Rory's eyes met hers and his head cocked. "Fourth of July!"

Grandpa's favorite holiday.

"There'll be concerts and parades and parties and fireworks . . ." Oops, Rory hated fireworks. "These are good fireworks. They shoot them from barges out in the bay. Ours are the best. The Washington Post says so."

Ours. After all these years, Kim still felt her town's desperate competition with the other two beaches. Tourist dollars were scarce and Osprey Beach lacked North Beach's antique shops and Chesapeake Beach's water park and resort. Without the annual designation of "best place to watch fireworks over the Bay," Grandpa and other Osprey Beach merchants would struggle for survival. Income from Independence Day sales were needed to carry Grandpa's store through the lazy summer into holiday gift-buying season.

So hurray for the fireworks. Rory would just have to adapt.

"Did I ever tell you about the summer Grandpa and I won the sand sculpture contest?" Okay, so she was babbling at a dog. The memories flooding her brain needed an outlet. Freud would love it.

"Several people sculpted adult sea turtles," she told Rory. "But we made baby turtles, fifty-one of them running from their nest into the water. They looked so real we had to keep the sea gulls away until the judges got to us!"

She smiled, remembering that lazy, happy summer. The last summer for childhood fun. The following year she entered Middle School, a hormone-laden nightmare where childhood friends metamorphosed into boy-chasing, blithering idiots.

The light turned green and she eased into traffic. Fifty yards later, brake lights flashed. Kim peered through the windshield and groaned. The Chesapeake Beach geese had waddled into the road, spreading across both lanes and stopping all traffic.

The car ahead of her honked. The geese turned beady eyes towards the offender but didn't move.

Kim sighed. The proper way to deal with the geese was to drift forward, if necessary bumping the ring leader with the car. Tourists, of course, didn't know this.

On the sidewalk beside her, a group of girls, maybe eleven or twelve years old, giggled and whispered as they watched three boys chase one another with snapping beach towels.

Kim winced and looked away, but images of the summer following her sand-sculpture win surfaced. Debbie Abrams and Beth Woods -- her best friends since elementary school -- strutting the boardwalk clad in tiny bikinis, giggling whenever some testosterone-crazed boy did something stupid. No, they didn't want to enter the egg-toss contest. No, they didn't want to go swimming. And, no, they most certainly did not want to sit around listening to some dumb band playing elevator music.

New images: The after-fireworks party complete with live D.J. Michael Todd, quarterback extraordinaire, asking her to dance. Debbie and Beth poking fun of her dancing, then later shunning her. Moping around Grandpa's store. Grandpa's confession of the bullies in his own childhood.

Behind her, someone leaned on a horn. As a group, the geese honked back but didn't yield an inch. Rory woofed and hung over the back seat.

"Yeah, I'm sure you'd do a good job of clearing the road," she told him. "Then we'd have the tourists mad at you for picking on the poor birds."

Poor birds, indeed. She watched a shop owner march into the road, brandishing a broom. The geese lined up facing her. The broom swung. The nearest geese skipped aside while their partners in crime maintained control of the two-lane road. Goose honks joined more car horns.

On the sidewalk, the clowning boys suddenly froze, noses pointed at a smaller boy shuffling from the water park. An official Mickey Mouse backpack hung from the boy's boney shoulders, Hawaiian-style swim trunks fell to knobby knees. He stared at his feet as he walked and didn't see the older boys until they surrounded him. The boy's eyes widened as the leader of the gang shoved him into another boy, who pushed him back toward the center of the circle. The leader's hand raised, fist clenched.

Kim threw the car into park and reached for the door handle. As she stepped out of the car, however, the shop owner descended on the boys. The bullies scattered, leaving the small boy alone and trembling. A slanting ray of light illuminated chubby, tear-streaked cheeks.

Biting her lip, Kim crawled back into the car. The boy wouldn't welcome a stranger's attention. An image surfaced. Another gang, another target. Grandpa, age eleven, newly arrived from Switzerland. Grandpa's confession.

Once upon a time, the confident, successful man she'd known all her life had been targeted by bullies. They ridiculed the way Grandpa dressed, snickered at his French accent, belittled his work ethic. When they discovered he couldn't swim, they tossed him into the bay. Like the boy on the sidewalk, Grandpa's only crime was being different.

Even after all the psychology classes explaining childhood angst, children's cruelty sickened her.

But they could also be useful, as

demonstrated by the trio of girls skipping down the sidewalk, waving slices of stale bread and calling "here ducky, ducky, ducky." Two sets of parents, arms laden with beach bags, wet towels and an open bag of bread, followed.

The geese turned towards the girls. Ah yes, tourist training 101.

The geese flocked around the children, clearing the road in seconds. And, mercy of mercies, the traffic light at the other end of Chesapeake Beach stayed green long enough for Kim to zip through.

She eased her grip on the wheel. In just a few minutes she'd get to hug Grandpa . . . and make him reveal whatever worried him.

The road turned inland and the bay briefly disappeared. A left turn onto Osprey Beach's First Avenue carried Kim back towards the water. As she passed Main Street, the boardwalk parking lot came into view. Normally empty at this time of the evening, the lot was dotted with Toyotas, Fords and even what looked like a black Mercedes.

Or was it a BMW? Kim sighed. Didn't matter anymore; she'd dumped the car-crazy boyfriend months ago.

Tapping the brake, she turned right onto the gravel alley that'd been the bane of her growing up years; after the third tumble from her new Schwinn destroyed the front wheel, she'd begun calling the pothole-laden street "bike-eating alley." It ran behind the backs of the houses and shops that lined the boardwalk. Small stones clinked against the van's undercarriage. Kim slowed, her eyes drawn to the tall, narrow homes that blocked her view of the bay.

Gone were the cottage bungalows of her childhood, the ones with the shops in the front, living quarters behind, postage-stamp yards out back. Hurricane Isabel's watery assault forced Grandpa and his neighbors to raise their homes above flood level. The new houses thrust three and four stories high, each floor sporting balconies with wonderful views of the bay, the bottom level reserved for garages or utility rooms that could survive hurricane induced floods.

The old cottages she'd loved were gone, but the bike-eating alley that dented bikes, flattened tires and lodged in knees and elbows remained.

As the car neared Grandpa's driveway, Kim shifted in her seat, conflicting emotions making it difficult to breathe. Excitement, concern, joy, apprehension, anticipation, dread.

The psychologist in her recognized the emotional tug-of-war as a classic response to returning home. But academic understanding didn't stop the turmoil in her gut.

The next few days would be stressful. Her

bossy aunts would descend and she needed to prevent them from pushing her around or triggering an angry outburst. She'd help Grandpa in the store, but needed to resist getting caught in the feeding frenzy that always surrounds diamonds. And Grandpa would push to make the current living arrangement permanent and she needed to that resist, too.

She groaned. Oh, to avoid the disappointment she'd see in Grandpa's eyes.

Especially after he'd gone ahead and renovated the top floor, turning three bedrooms and one bath into two luxurious master suites. He'd even fenced the back yard for Rory.

When Grandpa told her what he'd done, she'd pretended to share his enthusiasm. She accepted his offer to stay with him until her Oregon home sold; she couldn't afford to pay the mortgage and the high rents in College Park at the same time. But she'd warned Grandpa that her ultimate goal was to buy a house closer to the University of Maryland, where she'd be teaching in the fall. He'd responded with a "we'll see."

Grandpa didn't understand that after living on her own for ten years, the idea of sharing a place with anyone gave her chills. And she certainly couldn't tell him that his nosiness and matchmaking attempts would drive her crazy.

Whenever she visited him, he arranged for a succession of his buddies' sons to "drop in." Knowing her weakness for "bad boys" -- and her disastrous high school attraction to Jason White -- Grandpa carefully selected for the more wholesome: doctors, lawyers, business executives. Unfortunately, they'd all been too self-absorbed to notice their date's eyes glazing over.

His latest enthusiasm was a Pulitzer Prize winning journalist turned college professor. Grandpa had bombarded her with articles the man had written. Kim filed the stories away, unread. There was plenty of time to make her excuses.

While she could handle Grandpa's matchmaking, however, she was less efficient at quashing his dream that someday she'd join him as co-owner of Osprey Beach Jewelry. He couldn't understand her reluctance, her fear of being smothered by the large, extended family. Three aunts, eight cousins, all named after gemstones, all consumed by diamond fever . . . She shuddered to think she'd almost become one of them. One of the mindless masses dazzled by sparkle, blind to reality.

The job offer in Oregon had delayed that confrontation with Grandpa.

Now she was back in Maryland. Distance was no longer an excuse. The time for the painful confrontation loomed nearer.

Turning into Grandpa's driveway, she was surprised to see the garage door standing open. He must have just arrived.

She started to pull the van beside Grandpa's Camry, then noticed the open garden gate on her left. Now why would he enter through the backyard? From the garage, he could use the interior elevator to reach the living quarters above the shop. So why climb the outside stairs?

From the backseat, Rory whined. Probably needed to relieve himself.

She parked in the driveway, removed Rory's seatbelt and followed him into the backyard, closing the gate behind her. As she neared the outside staircase, she heard voices coming from the downstairs office.

Grandpa! And suddenly she was ten again, bounding up the steps two at a time, swinging open the screen door and . . .

Kim screeched to a halt, her mind trying to process what she saw. A figure dressed in black bent over a pile of clothes in front of Grandpa's workbench. The figure stood, turned towards her . . . Kim registered the ski mask, the snarled lips, the dilated eyes. Time slowed. He took a step, lifted his right hand. Something caught the office light, flashed . . . knife. He was raising a knife . . .

Rory sped by. Rear legs propelled him into the air. His mouth closed over the arm holding the weapon.

The man stumbled, roared and swung a battered briefcase. It caught Rory in the side. Fabric tore as the black dog dropped to the ground. The man raised the blood-spattered knife.

"No!"

Kim started for Rory, her feet slipping on the tiled floor. Oh god, oh god, she'd never make it in time. Tensing her muscles, she hurled her purse at the knife arm. It thunked against the blade, ripping the weapon from the assailant's fingers. The knife went flying.

The man swore and charged towards her. His free arm hit her shoulders and sent her sprawling. Feet thudded down the outside stairs.

Rory struggled to stand. Kim crawled to him, ran anxious hands down his sides. No blood, no protruding bones. He stood, shook himself and licked the right lens of her glasses.

Police. She needed police.

Pushing herself to her feet, she turned towards the phone on the workbench. Her eyes fell on the clothes. No, not clothes . . .Her heart stopped.

"Grandpa!"

Chapter 3

Grandpa lay on his side, his breath ragged, one hand clutched to his chest. Blood oozed between his fingers.

Dropping beside him, Kim stroked his face. Clammy. But he was alive.

"Grandpa?"

His eyes fluttered open, glassy, then focused on her. A small smile formed. He struggled to sit up. His fingers turned red with blood.

"No! Lay still." Whipping off her t-shirt, she pressed it against the wound. Grandpa groaned. But the blood flow slowed.

"Can you hold this in place for a minute?"

When he nodded and moved his hand onto the reddening cloth, Kim scrambled to her feet and snagged the portable phone. Fingers trembling, she reached for the 9, hit the 8 instead, no, no, no, punch the off, now, more slowly 9-1-1.

"My grandfather, he's been stabbed." The words came from her mouth, but she didn't recognize the squeaky voice. Taking a deep breath, she gave the emergency operator Grandpa's address.

"The house sits beside the boardwalk, so they'll need to drive down the alley that connects First and Second. Come in the back."

"I have an ambulance leaving Dunkirk right now."

Dunkirk. Fifteen minutes away if you drove the speed limit. Rory nudged Kim's arm. Kim glanced down, saying "Not now, swee . . ." Something glimmered in his mouth. The knife. Oh, gawd, he was carrying the knife.

Kim dropped the phone and lunged for Rory. Startled, he jumped out of her reach. Feet planted, tail up, he appeared ready to bolt. If he reached the interior stairs, she'd never catch him.

Pitching her voice low, she tried to calm the young dog. "It's okay, sweetie. Bring it here." Cooing softly, she extended her right hand. Rory's tail began to lower. Babbling nonsense, she took a step towards him. His tail raised.

Kim froze.

"Bring it, sweetie. You want a cookie?" Rory cocked his head. Slowly, Kim reached her left hand into a jeans pocket, found a dog treat, showed it to him. "Bring it here, sweetie."

Tension drained from the poodle's body. He trotted forward, laid the knife in the extended hand, accepted the cookie. She threw the knife onto the workbench, out of Rory's reach.

Rushing back to Grandpa, she dropped to her knees. His breath was ragged, but his eyes were open and alert. The t-shirt over his wound was solid red. Kim gently lifted his hand, prepared to continue applying pressure. But the blood had stopped flowing.

She stroked Grandpa's hand. "It's going to be okay. Ambulance should be here soon."

His skin was so gray, so cold. Maybe a blanket would help.

Grandpa grabbed her hand.

"Don't leave."

"But you need . . ."

"Need you here . . ."

Before she could protest, he reached into his suit coat pocket and pulled out a package of Swiss chocolates. He muttered something and passed the chocolate to Kim.

Where was that ambulance?

"Grandpa, lay still. You're going to start bleeding again."

But he ignored her, intent on extracting

something from the inside pocket of his coat.

"Here. Let me get it."

With a nod, he slumped to the floor. Kim opened his jacket, found the pocket and pulled out a small brown envelope. The kind jewelers used to carry gemstones.

"This it?" She held it up.

Grandpa nodded, pushed at her hand. "Hide."

Huh?

He pushed again. "Hide!"

He watched as she tucked the envelope into her jeans pocket, then grabbed her hand.

"Jim . . ."

"Shhhh. You need to preserve your strength."

Grandpa gripped her hand. Tight. "But . . ."

"Grandpa, please!"

Hearing the panic in her voice, he coughed and closed his eyes, murmuring "bossy . . ."

Were those sirens? Please, let those be sirens.

Grandpa's grip loosened. His hand fell to the ground, limp. Rory licked her tears.

"Grandpa? Grandpa, don't you dare die on me!"

ABOUT THE AUTHOR

Lynn Franklin's five-star mystery series brings to life gemstone history, legend and lore. From childhood, gemstones, writing and mysteries have been an integral part of Lynn's life. After 30 years of teaching and writing for newspapers, magazines and the internet, she became an accredited jewelry professional and began writing the Jeweler's Gemstone stories.

Although Lynn's books are set in the Chesapeake Bay area, researching her latest,

The Carolina Emerald, offered the rare opportunity to tour a privately owned commercial emerald mine. Lynn uses these kinds of experiences to draw her readers into a fictional world populated with strong characters, quirky relatives and endearing dogs.

To learn more about Lynn's adventures – from dancing with swallows to flunking out of the writers' police academy to wrestling with Empress Josephine (the antique rose, not Napoleon's wife) – go to **www.LynnFranklin.com** and sign up for her Diamond Digest.

CPSIA information can be obtained
at www.ICGtesting.com
Printed in the USA
FSHW020629171218
54523FS